THE

HOUSE

AT

758

Kathryn Berla

Amberjack Publishing
New York, New York

Amberjack Publishing
228 Park Avenue S #89611
New York, NY 10003-1502
http://amberjackpublishing.com

Publisher's Cataloging-in-Publication data

Names: Berla, Kathryn, author.
Title: The House at 758 / Kathryn Berla.
Description: New York, NY: Amberjack Publishing, 2017.
Identifiers: ISBN 978-1-944995-24-9 (pbk.) | 978-1-944995-37-9 (ebook) | LCCN 2017936251
Summary: Krista is still grieving the death of her mother when her father's new girlfriend moves into their home. Distancing herself from everyone around her, Krista spends all her time watching a mysterious house, the house at 758.
Subjects: LCSH Grief--Fiction. | Family--Fiction. | Mothers and daughters--Fiction. | Grandparents--Fiction. | Teenage girls--Fiction. | Teenagers--Fiction. | BISAC YOUNG ADULT FICTION / General
Classification: LCC PZ7.B45323 Ho 2017 | DDC [Fic]—dc23

Cover Design: Theresa Evangelista

For Eugen

Chapter | 1

The house wasn't hard to find. In this neighborhood, all the numbers are spray painted in black right onto the concrete curb. Even though the curb is cracked and crumbling in places, the numbers are bold and distinct. The paint still looks fresh.

From the side mirror of my car, which is parked across the street and down two houses, I have an unobstructed view. A black tar roof sags over one side of the tiny home. Underneath it, a green and white-striped awning hangs above a medium-sized picture window. Once upon a time it must have been a cheerful splash of color that complemented the pale green walls of the house. But now there are gaping holes in the awning, and it can't even hold back the sun.

I want to get a better look, so I pull up a little closer, wary of being noticed by someone who will realize I don't belong.

Even my car doesn't belong here. It's much nicer and newer than the other cars I can see. I call it "The

1

Hornet" for its bright yellow color and black trim. My father gave it to me for my sixteenth birthday, and for a while we both pretended it made me happy, but it didn't.

In the beginning, it was a welcome distraction. I drove everywhere those first few weeks—to the beach, to the city, along the narrow, winding road that leads to the top of the mountain. My father didn't care where I went. He was just glad to see me get out of the house, get out of my head, do something on my own for a change—on my own initiative without someone pushing me to do it. But after a while, the spell was broken. No matter where I went, there I was, just like before.

But my father didn't have this problem. He had moved on with his life. He didn't need a new car or anything else. It happened just like that. One day we were like two planets orbiting around the same sun—granted it was a miserable sun, but we were there together, and we understood each other even if we didn't have much to say during those days. Then the next thing I knew, my father sort of spun out of my orbit and went on with his life, and I was alone. The only person who could feel what I felt and knew what I knew . . . well, he had other plans for his life, and I couldn't hitch a ride with him. Maybe he wanted me to; I'm sure he did. But I couldn't and still don't understand how he could just move forward.

I wonder what my father would think if he knew where I was right now. He wouldn't consider me brave—nobody would. Although, it's taken me weeks to work up the courage to steer the Hornet through these streets. A few times I've gotten within a block of this house before turning back. Today I finally made it all the way. I feel like I've done the courageous thing by coming here, even if nobody else realizes it. I'm doing the necessary thing that no one else will do.

The house is plainly in my line of sight. The windows are open, and a hopeless breeze plays with the curtains, teasing its occupants. I rest my cheek against the driver's side window. It's cool against my skin, and an icy flow from the air conditioner aims straight at my face. It's already five o'clock in the afternoon, and I can sense the heat on the other side of the glass. Most of the lawns in this neighborhood have turned brown. The sidewalks are empty. Even the children are absent. They must be waiting for the temperature to drop before venturing outside to play.

On the street in front of the house a huge crow pecks at the guts of a squirrel flattened into the pavement. It's having a tough time since the juicy parts have already been baked into the asphalt.

Further down the street, a young man with a shaved head walks toward me. He's wearing a white tank top and loose khaki pants. He's plugged into a music source hidden inside his pocket. He moves with a beat in his step and seems oblivious to the heat—like the last person on earth in one of those post-apocalyptic movies.

The guy is coming closer. In minutes, he'll pass by my car and wonder about the strange girl behind the wheel of the yellow Beetle. I don't belong here and he'll know that right away. But I remind myself I don't have to explain my presence to him or anyone else. I'm entitled to be here as much as he is.

Underneath the green and white-striped awning, a shadow moves behind the window. I strain my eyes to see, but then it's gone. Maybe it was never there.

Are they home? What are they doing right now? Can they see me? The screen door is open but contains no screen. The house looks like it's given up on the people inside. In front, a frail, sickly tree leans to one side. Underneath it, a patch of green—weeds that somehow survive in its shade. This place is exactly as I'd always imagined one thousand times before.

It's getting late. My father will be wondering where I am right now. Marie's cooking for us tonight—*coq au vin*—and I know I'm expected to be amazed by it and shower her with gratitude for all the effort she put into it. As if cooking a dinner with a French name is supposed to give you special status or give you rights to attention over everyone else. But I don't care about her *coq au vin* or any other fancy thing she decides to cook. Instead of eating *coq au vin* and pretending everything's just fine, my dad should be here with me.

Strangely enough, despite my nervousness, I'm quite hungry and my stomach rumbles at the thought of a burger. Maybe some fries as well. Dinner isn't until six o'clock, so I can stop at the drive-through and still get home before it's on the table.

The young man walks by my car and turns his head to look in my window. He nods at me and I smile back. He's close enough that I can see the tattoos on his arm—some kind of flag I don't recognize and a chain link bracelet around his bicep. I want to turn my head to see the tattoo on his neck, but I don't dare. Soon he's past my car and on his way to somewhere else.

I take one last look at the house before leaving. The numbers on the curb are out of place. They're bold, black, and fresh, and remind me of the last soldiers at a fort everyone else has already abandoned. 7-5-8. I know I'll be back.

Chapter | 2

The next day I wake to a morning so beautiful, that for a few minutes, my life feels sparkling and new and full of promise. As though a hairline crack in my consciousness has opened, I remember this sensation, and it feels so ancient it's almost like déjà vu—like when something comes over you that can only be explained by a past life. The sky is liquid blue and the air so clear I can see outlines of buildings twenty miles away. I wish I knew how to hold onto this feeling and make it mine forever. But the moment passes quickly like the breeze from the wings of a butterfly—barely there and then not there at all.

My eyes wander to Mt. Diablo in the east. Like a giant's fist punched upward through the earth's crust, it rules over the cowering hills that surround it. In school, we learned the Spaniards named it when a village of runaway mission Native Americans disappeared into its shadow. As if the devil tricked them to protect the innocents.

I find it comforting. It's solid and constant, and the winds of time have done nothing more than smooth its rough edges. The Miwok Native Americans believed it to be the birthplace of the world and their people. I tell myself that, in contrast, my life is insignificant. Others were here before me. Others have suffered worse. When I look at the mountain, I can practically feel the hot breath of the pursuing Spanish soldiers. I imagine the panicked Native Americans running through the weeds, sharp stones cutting their bare feet, willing themselves to vanish with fear and death always less than a step behind them.

LYLA'S COMING, so I need to get up and get ready. I climb out of my red pop-up tent and zip it shut. Lyla jokes that I'm crawling back into the womb and maybe she's right, but I don't care. My tent is my refuge; I feel safe up here. The day that Marie moved her stuff into our house, I moved into the tent on top of the garage. I've been living in it for six weeks now. At night when my light is on, it glows like a ruby.

When I was younger, my family would come up here to watch the Fourth of July fireworks which are miles away. Sometimes when there was a full moon, we'd carry up thermoses of hot chocolate and just sit and talk and laugh. My father had a ladder installed that securely attached to the side of the house so we could get up and down quite easily. My mom used to call it our Swiss Family Robinson treehouse, because you can practically reach out and touch the branches of a giant oak. But the word "family" no longer applies. It's

7

just my treehouse now.

At night, I watch the owls come to life and glide silently to their favorite lookout posts. One night, a massive great-horned owl perched just outside my tent, only inches from me. For an hour we shared the same space. I imagined it was clearing the fog of sleep from its head and planning the night while I was preparing for bed.

When I climb down the ladder I can see that my father's car is still in the driveway which seems strange until I realize it's Tuesday. He doesn't start seeing patients until eleven o'clock on Tuesdays. Hopefully Marie went in early to open. She used to be his nurse, but now she runs his practice. In a way, she also runs our lives.

"Krista!" Dad says with a nervous smile when I walk into the kitchen. I can tell something's on his mind, and he's trying to find a way to bring it up. "How's the air up there?" he chuckles.

"Fine." I reach for a box of cereal from the shelf.

"I was thinking I could make you breakfast this morning." Now I know something's up.

"That's okay. Lyla's coming over and we're going to hang out today."

"I thought she was going to Maine for the summer."

"She's leaving tomorrow so this will be our last chance to do something until school starts."

Even in his pajamas, Dad always looks put together and in control.

"Have you thought any more about how you're going to occupy yourself this summer?" he asks. *This is what's on his mind?*

"Nope." I crunch my cereal, trying to shut out the conversation.

"Well, you probably still have time if you want to reconsider swim team," he says.

"Been there, done that." *Where's Lyla?*

"Krista, don't be rude. I'm trying to have a serious conversation." His upper lip tightening the way it does when he's mad is the only thing that betrays his loss of control.

"I'm not being rude. I just don't want to do swim team," I answer with my mouth full, and a few drops of milk land on the table.

"Then you're going to have to get a job. Or take a class. Or do something for God's sake!"

I don't respond. How can I? I don't want to do anything. Right now, all I want to do is zip myself back into my tent.

"Marie worked really hard to make a nice dinner for you last night and you hardly ate anything."

So this is what's really bothering him. The rest was just prologue.

"Am I supposed to force myself to eat if I'm not hungry?" I don't mention the burger and fries I had on the way home. Maybe I did it on purpose—so what? The doorbell rings, and I push my chair back to get up, but Dad beats me to it.

"I'll get it," he says and I detect a warning in his voice. "You stay and finish your breakfast."

He returns to the kitchen with Lyla gliding behind him. With her silky black hair and flawless, tanned skin, I often wonder if she's ever had a negative thought in front of a mirror. Lyla generally dresses in bold colors,

9

and today she's wearing emerald green. Her lithe, delicate grace has always made me feel gangly and awkward, although she always claims my athleticism makes her feel like a wuss.

"What are you girls up to today?" I know Dad's trying to be friendly, but I wish he'd leave us alone on our last day together.

"I'm not sure, Dr. Matzke," she chirps. "What do you want to do, Krista?"

"We'll figure something out, I'm sure."

"Dinner's at six," he says. "We'll pick up something on the way home. Lyla, will you be joining us?" Dad is just as fearful of her being gone all summer as I am. He knows she keeps me grounded.

"Um, I'd better check with my parents first. Can I let you know this afternoon?"

"Of course. And Krista, just text Marie once Lyla knows . . . and don't forget to brush your teeth," he absurdly adds.

"Yes, Dad. I'm almost seventeen. I know how to brush my teeth, and I already brushed."

"You brushed before breakfast?" His upper lip tightens again. "How does that make any sense?"

Control freak!

"Just leave me alone, please, Dad."

Lyla shifts uncomfortably in her seat and stares out the window as if willing herself to be outside this room. It hurts me to see her react this way because if she can't handle a little bit of harmless bickering between me and my dad, how could she ever handle what's going on inside my head? And if not Lyla, then who? For sure not Dad anymore.

My father picks up my empty cereal bowl and puts it in the sink. He turns on the tap. "By the way, your grandfather is coming next week," he says. "He's been feeling a little under the weather, so he's coming for a check-up."

"Grandpa's coming all the way from Venezuela to see a doctor?" I ask.

"The doctors are better over here," he says. "He called this morning and I told him he's welcome to stay with us for as long as it takes."

"What's wrong with him?"

I hardly know my grandfather. Even before they moved to Venezuela, Grandma was the focal point of their visits. His thick Hungarian accent made it difficult for us to communicate. But Grandma is gone now. Mom too. I guess we're his only next-of-kin, as they say, even though Dad's not a blood relation. I wonder what my grandfather will think about Marie living here. I can't imagine he'll like it any more than I do.

"It's not all that easy to understand him over the phone, but I'm sure it's nothing," Dad says. "Maybe he just wants to come see you. It must be lonely for him these days."

"PLEASE TELL ME we don't have to hang out in your tent today." Lyla's not a big fan of the tent. She's a girly-girl and I'm exactly the opposite, whatever that is. When I was younger, Lyla used to call me a tomboy. Coming from anyone else I would have taken it as an insult, but Lyla always said it like she was proud of me.

"It's okay," I reassure her. "Nobody's home for the

rest of the day. We can go up to my room."

"Thank God. It's like one hundred degrees out there. Or will be soon." We go up the stairs to my bedroom. My clothes still fill the drawers and the closet, and I still use the bathroom, but I've moved all my favorite things to the tent. I even have a fan there.

"Do you mind if I do my nails?" Lyla retrieves a small bottle of nail polish from her purse. She sets to work without waiting for my response. "Krista, what are you going to do this summer?"

"Stop sounding like my dad."

"I'm sorry but you seriously make me worry. Living up in that tent all by yourself. Why don't you hang out with Sissy and Grace this summer while I'm gone?"

"Sissy and Grace? Please."

"Don't act like you're better than them, Krista. You need to have more than one friend."

"Relax. I don't think I'm better than anyone. I just have nothing in common with them, that's all."

"It's just . . . it's a big responsibility for me when I go away."

"How so?"

"I mean . . ." she stammers. "You know. I just worry and want you to be happy."

"And being pushed off on Sissy and Grace will make me happy? They're your friends, Lyla. Not mine."

"I'm not pushing you off, Krista. Don't say that. You're the one who pushes people away. If I didn't care so much about you then why would I be worrying so much?"

"Well, I'm sorry I'm such a big responsibility. And you don't have to worry about me. I can take care of myself."

"You know I didn't mean it that way." Lyla looks hurt. "We'll always be best friends. It's just that . . . you don't always have to have a lot in common with someone to be their friend. Look at us . . . friends since second grade and we're really different from each other. Just be a little more open to others, that's all I'm saying."

In my head, I know she's right, but how do you go from A to B? It's easy to say it and understand it, but the other part . . . that's not so easy. But I know Lyla well enough to know she feels bad having to spell it out for me like this. Right now, she probably feels she pushed me too hard. Lyla and I have history so it's easy with her. With everyone else it seems like too much of an effort.

"Let me do your hair for you!" Her voice suddenly sounds bright.

Ninety minutes later my long, brown hair is sleek and shiny with loose curls that tumble gently over my shoulders like in the magazines. How does she do it? My mother used to say my hair had a mind of its own, but if I would be patient with it, it would always behave perfectly. I used to wonder if she was really talking about me and not my hair. I usually get around to figuring things out if I have enough time.

Lyla calls her parents who give their permission for her to eat dinner at our house but she has to be home by eight. Whenever I think my dad is too controlling I think about Lyla's parents. I couldn't stand a day under their rules but Lyla seems to enjoy the tight constraints they put on her. That's another way we're different.

"I have to wake up super early tomorrow so I can't

stay late," she informs me, and it sounds like she's making an excuse for their overprotectiveness because she knows how I feel. "What should we do now? Our hair is done. Our nails are done and we look hot, girl! Let's go unleash ourselves on the world." She beams at me like I'm her marvelous creation.

"I have an idea," I say. "Let's take the Hornet."

"ARE YOU GOING to tell me what we're doing here?" Lyla sounds irritable. The "surprise" that I promised looks less and less promising. "I don't even know where we are and I don't think my parents would be very happy if they knew I was here . . . wherever we are." Her green silk top is rumpled and . . . *is that actually a sweat stain under her arm?*

"This is the house." I point across the street to 758. "In case you're interested."

A dark-haired, young boy bounces a ball against the garage door. Pound-bounce-catch. Pound-bounce-catch. It makes a racket each time it hits the cheap vinyl door.

"Oh my God!" Lyla's mouth forms an O of horror. "This is a new low. We shouldn't be here, Krista. Let's go."

I don't know what I was expecting. Of course she wouldn't understand why I brought her here. Why would she? I barely understand it myself.

Just then, the front door opens, and a woman walks out. She speaks loudly to the boy in a foreign language. The boy looks dejected and catches the ball on the bounce. He walks over to the dead grass of the tiny front lawn and throws the ball up in the air and then catches it. He does it again. The woman walks back to the front door and then turns to look at the Hornet. She stares for a few seconds before disappearing into the house.

"She saw us, Krista. I mean it, let's get out of here." Lyla's voice is panicky. It doesn't take much to make her nervous. "This is so wrong."

I pull away from the curb and drive slowly by the house. The woman looks out the window as we pass by.

For the rest of the night, Lyla is different. She's quiet through dinner and I wonder if my father notices the change. She also keeps looking at me as though she's noticing something for the first time, and it makes me wonder what that something is. I know there's nothing new inside me. It's only that I've gotten good at hiding what's already there. I took her to the house hoping that she might get it, but I should have known better. Nobody does.

After dinner, I walk Lyla to her car, but we don't say too much, and we don't talk about what happened earlier. We say goodbye and hug each other tightly. She tells me to take care of myself and that she's only a phone call away. There are promises to celebrate our birthdays when she gets back from Maine. I stay for a moment longer to watch the red taillights of her car disappear down the road along with the sparkle that is Lyla's life.

Chapter | 3

The dream I'm having doesn't want to let me go, and I don't want to let go of it either. When I open my eyes, I've forgotten everything except the feeling, which is warm and satisfying, so I close my eyes hoping to return to that place. I'm usually able to sleep through the typical morning sounds, but a baby's outraged cries are new and succeed in waking me. The Sullivans must have brought their baby home. It seems impossible this day could finally be here after everything that led up to it.

Mom spent hours supporting Rachel Sullivan during a very difficult time. Together, they drove to fertility specialists when Mr. Sullivan was out of town on business, my mom taking notes for him while the doctors explained this reason or that reason the Sullivans couldn't conceive. And then came the long, drawn out process of adoption—more difficult for the Sullivans because they weren't young anymore. Mom helped with that as well. It was an exciting time for all of us, but now I can't remember how that felt.

The baby is finally here. I can hear its howls, and I sympathize. It can't be easy to be tiny and helpless and still attempt to make sense of everything life throws at you. I just wish Mom was here to see it. That would have made her happy. Maybe I should go next door and visit them soon. Mom would have wanted me to.

Lying here on my foam pad with a thin sheet loosely covering me, I can feel my hair—long, thick and damp with sweat—around my throat. My scrunchie came loose while I slept and now I feel like I'm being strangled by hair. There's no more delaying, so I get up and crawl out of my tent. It's already hot, and by the position of the sun, it seems I've slept late.

I think of Lyla relaxing on the plane, maybe reading a book or watching a movie, thinking about a lazy summer on the beautiful coast of Maine. I went with her once, when we were younger, and her grandparents were also younger and willing to allow her to bring a friend. I remember a formal, gray stone manor with a wide, green lawn that spilled into the ocean behind it. We sat in lounge chairs under the shade of a tree and read silly books and told each other silly stories of what we would be when we grew up, and who we would marry. When we got hot we ran into the salty water and splashed the stickiness off our sunburned skin. Her grandmother served us oatmeal cookies and huge, sweating plastic tumblers of lemonade.

Now Lyla's grandparents want her for themselves, and I think I understand why even though it's hard for me to be left behind. They only see her a few times a year and those times grow more and more precious the older they get. I guess when you're old you probably realize how important it is to focus on the people you love. At some point, you must know that tomorrow might never come. I never used to get that, like most kids my age. But when you do finally get around to understanding it . . . well then you just wish you hadn't.

The back door is unlocked, so I don't have to pull the key from its hiding place under the smooth, oval rock in the rose bed. The morning dishes and coffee cups are still in the sink—I make a mental note to take care of that so as not to give Marie another reason to complain, as if she needs one. There's a note stuck to the refrigerator door:

> Krista, dinner at 6. Please don't be late. Also, please set aside time to talk after dinner.

Dad, the obsessive scheduler.

I pull a bowl from the cupboard and walk into the pantry for cereal. A pathetic squawk like a crow with a belly-ache floats across the emptiness of the house. It's Charlie. Hardly anyone pays attention to him anymore. He was Mom's cockatiel, and all his physical needs are being met, but nobody can bear to do any more than just that. I set down the box of cereal and walk into the study. Charlie's cage stands alone in a corner next to the window.

"Hey boy," I say. "How're you doing?"

He cocks his head to get a better angle on me. He squawks in a disinterested way. Charlie has managed to pull every feather out of his chest and under his wings. The exposed pink skin repulses me, and I fight the impulse to look away. The bird vet said there was nothing medically wrong with Charlie. We even bought him new toys to cheer him up, but he doesn't find any joy in them. The vet said that birds are highly sensitive to their surroundings and will feel things that might not be visible to an outside observer. A canary will die in a coal mine long before the miners are aware of any toxic fumes.

After breakfast, another long, blank day is facing me. I go upstairs for a shower and decide to style my hair just like Lyla did yesterday. I've made a resolution to move my life forward in a positive direction. I will be forward thinking like Lyla. Then I'll sit down at my desk and plan for the rest of the summer. When Dad calls me in for his talk after dinner I will preempt whatever he says with my own plan. He'll be surprised at first and then pleased that I'm taking charge of my life. He'll back down and defer to whatever idea I come up with. He'll be amazed at the change in me. I'll start with my hair, though. After all, a person's outward appearance tells a lot about what's going on inside their head.

After my shower, I sit on the vanity chair in my bedroom armed with blow dryer, flat iron, wide-toothed comb, round brush, and curling iron.

A row of products is lined up in front of me: de-frizz leave-in conditioner, mousse, shine-enhancing oil, and hairspray. I try to remember the order and location on my head that Lyla used them. I carefully pin up my hair and start to work segment by segment. Less than halfway through, my arms are aching from the effort of holding the strands of hair away from my head. The result is not impressive. My hair looks flat and dull—probably because I've used too much product. The curls look limp and heavy, nothing like the shiny bouncy curls that Lyla created yesterday.

Two years ago, I was well on my way to becoming popular. Honestly, I was riding on Lyla's coattails, but still, I got lots of attention and invitations to great parties. I never doubted it would only keep getting better. It's hard for me to see that girl when I look at myself in the mirror today. I sigh and pull my hair into a ponytail.

I've had a minor setback but I'm still determined to look forward. I pull a notebook from my desk drawer and start writing a list.

Possible Summer Activities

I think about kids I know at school and the kinds of things they do in the summer.

Babysitting
Swim team
SAT prep classes
Summer abroad
Music camp
Retail (good discounts on clothes)
Start my own business (what kind of business?)

My post-breakfast enthusiasm begins to wane and I draw cartoon owls below the list. I wonder what Dad will suggest in our talk tonight.

I think about Lyla again and decide to call her tonight—or maybe just text her. I remember what she said yesterday. I'm a "big responsibility" for her, an emotional responsibility. I don't want to be a buzzkill and intrude on her excitement, bring her down during her vacation. I guess I'll just text.

Last summer it wasn't hard to lose my best friend for two months. I was still feeling numb and her absence was just one more thing I didn't care about. Last summer my father cut me a lot of slack and didn't say a word when I spent most of it in front of the TV. He didn't demand that I look for a way to occupy myself. He was barely taking care of himself and probably didn't notice a lot of what I did. Last summer Marie didn't live with us, either.

Now my feelings are returning. Just like a deep flesh wound that severs the nerves and leaves the surrounding flesh with no feeling. Then the nerves regenerate. They find their missing counterparts on the other side of the wound. They make new pathways. Slowly but surely, sensation returns to the flesh around the wound. My feelings are returning. Is that a good thing? It depends which feelings I'm having on any particular day. Most days I miss the numbness.

I have a stack of books on my desk—summer reading for my AP English class. How could my father accuse me of wasting my time if I manage to finish a book by the time he gets home? Or at least put a serious dent in one. But I know what I'm going to do, so who am I kidding? I'm going to the only place where I don't have to hide what I feel. I'm going back to 758.

THE DRIVE TAKES thirty minutes, but this time I don't have to plug the address into my navigation system. I find my way easily, and soon I'm parked in the same spot facing away from the house. I've adjusted my side and rear mirrors to get a good view. There's a car in the driveway that wasn't there before—an old, brown Toyota. The paint is so faded that silver patches are showing through. If it wasn't here yesterday, then it probably doesn't belong to the woman I saw who I'm sure is the mother. I'm guessing it's *his,* and maybe I'll see him today. My heart starts to thump hard in my chest, so I pick out a playlist on my phone to relax me, and then I slouch down in my seat to wait.

After about ten minutes, I glance at my gas gauge and notice it's near empty. I could turn off the engine to save on gas, but heat waves rise visibly from the street and my air conditioning won't cool unless the engine is running. It seems like I should go, but before I have a chance to reposition my mirrors, there's a rap on my window. A policeman stands there motioning for me to roll down the window, which I do.

"Driver's license and registration," he says.

I reach in the glove compartment and pull out the plastic pouch containing all my paperwork. I fumble around in my purse for my driver's license. "Is there a problem?" I ask.

He's young and looks sympathetic. With pale hair that clings to his scalp from perspiration, and cheeks flushed with heat, he doesn't quite fit my idea of what a cop should look like. His eyes are blue and kind, but he holds himself with a posture of authority.

"Can I ask what you're doing here?" he wants to know.

"Am I doing something illegal?" I ask. "It's a public street." He peers at my driver's license.

"No, you're not doing anything illegal. Wait here for a moment, please." He walks back to his car with my license and gets in. I turn off my engine to conserve gas. A few minutes later he returns and hands me my license.

"Look, why don't you move along?" he says. "We received a call from a resident. You're making them nervous. Apparently, this isn't your first time here."

I don't know how to respond. I want to argue with him since technically I'm not breaking the law, but I know enough not to argue with a cop. For some reason I feel humiliated, but why should I? I foolishly ask him where the nearest gas station is, and he points me in the direction. We both pull away from the curb at the same time, and I swear I see a shadow behind the window underneath the striped awning.

With the Hornet filled up with gas, I'm restless—purposeless. I can't get past the feeling of humiliation. The policeman acted as though *I* had done something wrong. I wanted to tell him it isn't me . . . I've done nothing wrong. *Just go up to that house*, I wanted to say. *758. Knock on the door. Talk to the person who answers, and let them explain who's done something wrong. Not me who's just parked on a public street.*

I'm embarrassed and angry at the same time. I can't bring myself to go home but I have nowhere else to go, so I drive aimlessly until I'm within blocks of the mall. The mall seems as good a place to be as any. I can cool off there. And be anonymous.

Kids from my school don't come to this mall. There's an outdoor mall closer to my home that has fountains and palm trees and posh little shops where women with oversized Chanel sunglasses and Marc Jacobs purses leisurely window-shop, lattes in hand. This mall, on the other hand, is serious and fully enclosed. The architecture isn't all that welcoming, but the message is clear: *Come inside these doors to shop and buy. Stay as long as you like—as long as it takes.* Personally, I have no desire to shop, even though my father gave me a credit card of my own. I pull into the multi-level parking structure where the Hornet will stay cool. There's a food court in this mall—and no one would ever consider asking a girl who's lingering over lunch to move along.

THE MALL SHOPPERS remind me of salmon swimming upstream, and I join their numbers. I'm swept up in their single-mindedness, which appeals to me in its simplicity. I pass by stores . . . children's shoes, yoga clothing, giant pretzels, gourmet chocolate, sporting goods. I pause in front of the sporting goods store. The mannequins in the display window are dressed in brightly-colored fleece jackets, nylon sweatpants, and hiking boots. The male figure carries an elaborate orange and black camping backpack. The female wears a broad-brimmed canvas sun hat. Her head has been twisted slightly and angled to give her the appearance of looking up at her male companion. Maybe he's just told a joke or maybe he's giving her directions or warning about rattlesnakes and bears. Each of her hands clasps a walking pole. Their faces are black and smooth—featureless. Their world in this glass display case is still innocent and pure. I walk into the store.

I'm not much for sports or even outdoor equipment, but I know there's something here for me. I walk through aisles of dumbbells and athletic socks and yoga mats. I even pause to consider a pair of pink and gray running shoes, impractical for what I'm about to do.

Then I see what it is I've been looking for: a monocular. Small, black, portable, only about four inches long. I bring the lens to my eye and focus on the other side of the store. A sign that says *On Sale Today Only!* is plainly visible, as though it was directly in front of me. From my rooftop tent, I would have the eyesight of a great-horned owl. I barely hesitate before dropping it into my purse.

Inside the wallet in my purse is my own personal credit card. I can pay for the monocular but I won't. I'm committed to it now and just knowing that gives me the same feeling I've had in the past, my heart so full and my senses sharp and finely tuned. It's as though I've just taken the biggest, coldest breath of air that completely fills me to the last fiber of my most insignificant nerve ending. But I know from experience the feeling will morph into a cold, sick shame before I walk out the door, so why am I doing it again? With my head down, I walk away from the aisle where others have now come to browse.

I've almost reached the entrance of the store when I raise my head and look straight into the face of a boy I know from school. He wears a badge that identifies him as an employee of the store. Jake. I know Jake Robbins, or know of him, even though we've never spoken. He plays football, and I see him at lunch with other jocks who are popular and who hang around the starry-eyed, glossy-haired girls whom life seems to favor. I'm not sure if Jake is popular because boys move more easily in and out of different social groups at our school. But he has everything a boy would need to achieve top social status. He's handsome. He's athletic.

And now he's looking right at me . . . and shaking his head ever so slightly. He has a look on his face that says *don't do this*. And, without breaking eye contact, I walk straight to the door and exit the store.

Back out in the mall I'm on the shopper treadmill once again and the monocular in my purse seems like it's sending out a distress signal. It feels like a hundred-pound weight is pulling the strap of my purse down hard against my shoulder. My stomach churns and I know I only have minutes to locate a bathroom. At the end of the mall there's a Cineplex theater which I race toward to buy a ticket for a movie I've never heard of. When I enter the lobby, I run to the bathroom where I empty both my stomach and bowels within seconds. I've lost my nerve and I know I'll never be able to pull this off again. It's my first time being caught. Lyla said I'd hit a new low. Now I know I've hit another one.

The dark theater is almost empty and previews are already playing. I put my feet up on the seat in front of me and unzip my purse. My hand searches for the monocular and curls around it. It feels hard and dangerous, like a grenade. I zip up my purse and stare at the screen. The preview that's playing is supposed to be funny but the actor has a cruel expression. I scrunch down further in my seat and slide my feet, one on top of the other, into the gap between the seats in front of me. I'm so tired I can barely keep my eyes open. The image of the cop with the gentle eyes comes back to me. *Move along*.

Chapter | 4

My cell phone wakes me. *How long have I been asleep?* Two older women are seated three seats down from me in the still almost empty theater. They seem disgusted by the interruption and cluck to each other. My phone chimes again, and I pull it from my purse. The screen glows and lights up the space around me. The two women make a huge production of rising from their seats and relocating to the row in front of me, shaking their heads in disapproval. The funny thing is they don't even know how right they are. I'd move away from me too if I were them . . . but not just because of my disruptive cell phone. I have two text messages.

Dad:

> Happy Birthday! Don't be late for dinner

Lyla:

Happy Birthday! BFFs 4ever 4ever!

It's my birthday. I'm seventeen.
Happy birthday, loser.

It's SIX THIRTY when I finally pull into my driveway. Dad will be upset, but he won't say anything because it's my birthday. Marie will be busy in the kitchen speaking sweetly to my dad and pretending that everything is fine but, in reality, she'll be mad. But I'm counting on that birthday protective shield where nobody's allowed to show their anger. Sometimes I don't know what bothers me more . . . Marie taking my father away from me, or Marie trying to take *me* away from me. Most of the time I just wish she'd leave me alone and quit trying to insert herself into my life. Even Dad doesn't try to do that as much anymore.

I don't think Dad has any idea how far in over his head he is. Sometimes I actually feel sorry for him. He wants both Marie and me to be happy but that can't happen. One of us is going to be disappointed if the other one has her way. But I'm surprised when I walk into the kitchen where I hear their voices and they both look up at me with genuine happiness in their faces.

"Happy Birthday, kiddo!" Dad says. He walks over to give me a two-armed hug. I can't remember the last time that's happened.

"Happy Birthday, Krista!" Marie holds up an elaborately decorated chocolate cake. "I wish I could have made one for you myself, but I didn't have enough time."

"It's the sentiment that counts," Dad interjects.

"Thanks." I know Dad thinks I resent the cake and maybe I do. This is my first ever store-bought cake because last year I had no cake at all even though my father bought me the Hornet. A birthday cake is a much more complicated thing than a car, and last year neither one of us was ready to tackle it. But now I guess we're moving on, store-bought or not.

"Look, they started to spell my name with a 'C'." I point to the bright yellow icing cursive which has been smeared with chocolate frosting to turn the 'C' into a 'K'.

Dad looks over quickly at Marie to see if she's wounded by my remark, but all I can think of is how he should have planned a birthday dinner for just the two of us. It is *my* birthday, and he's worrying about *her*. I doubt Marie enjoys this any more than I do, so why not one more year to get used to birthdays before she joins us? One more year would have been nice.

Dinner is take-out Chinese in my honor. I'm surprisingly hungry, but then I remember that my stomach has been completely empty since I threw up at the theater. And I remember the monocular in my bag. It feels like a fat, ugly toad I want to poke with a stick until it hops away.

"Make a wish," Marie urges when she brings out the cake all glittering with tiny, pink candles. I wish the monocular would disappear. I wish I had this day to do over again.

After we've all had a slice of birthday cake, my father reminds me we've scheduled a talk, so we excuse ourselves to go to the bedroom he shares with Marie. The one he used to share with Mom. Marie stays behind in the kitchen to clean up.

"I've been thinking," Dad begins cautiously. "It might be a little much for you to plan things out right now, but I still think it's important for you to keep busy."

Where is this leading? With my father, you never know because he feels completely comfortable road-mapping other people's lives. Years of being a doctor has turned him into a control freak—or maybe he was just born that way. I can see how it could be reassuring to his patients who just want someone to tell them what to do. But I learned a long time ago it's better to see where he's going before responding, so I just nod my head noncommittally.

"So what I've decided . . ."

One part of the question has just been answered. I won't have a say in the decision.

". . . is that you'll be in charge of taking care of your grandpa when he's here."

"What does that mean?"

"It means that you'll be driving him to all his medical appointments and basically making sure he's entertained and gets his meals until we come home at night," Dad explains. "On the weekends, of course, I'll spell you a bit. And Marie will pitch in when she can. But it's mainly going to be up to you. Can I count on you, kiddo?" He gives a half-hearted chuckle and a light playful punch on my upper arm, the way he used to when I was little and about to run out on the soccer field. Poor Dad, I'm sure he wanted a boy.

"How do I entertain him?" I ask. "Half the time I can't even understand what he's saying."

The one thing I do remember about Grandpa is that he's not like other grandpas. There's always been a sort of invisible wall between us. Not so much a language barrier but more a barrier that has to do with oceans I've never crossed and continents I've never seen. At some point, we seem to have agreed to just be mysteries to each other and to carry on our relationship through his wife, my grandma, and my mom, his daughter. Now that they're both gone I wonder if we'll have anything to say to each other.

"You'll figure it out. And anyway, the important thing is to make sure he's on time to his doctors' appointments and that he gets fed. Do it for Mom . . . remember, this is her dad. Wouldn't you want your daughter to take care of me if I was old and help-less?"

I find that image to be too disturbing so I put it out of my mind.

"Fine. I can handle it." I know I'm getting off easy. This is better than a real job and it will keep Dad off my case this summer. Or at least for as long as Grandpa stays.

"Another thing . . ." I guess Dad isn't finished yet. "Marie just found out she has the kids this weekend so we're flying down to Disneyland. Why don't you come? It will be good for you to get away."

I'd rather break both of my legs. Marie and Dad probably need a babysitter so they can go out for drinks at night. A weekend with those two brats stuck in a hotel room? But I know that's not completely fair. They probably resent my dad as much as I resent their mom.

"Do I have to decide right now?" I know what my

answer will be but I want Dad to think I'm at least considering the possibility.

"We'll need to buy your ticket tomorrow so let me know before I leave for work."

I figure it's safe to leave now but Dad has one more thing on his mind. He walks over to his bedside table and picks up a gift-wrapped box that he hands to me.

"Happy Birthday, Krista," he says softly. I think I hear sadness and regret in his voice.

"Thanks Dad." I gently peel away the wrapping paper to reveal the box underneath. A pair of binoculars.

"They're digital," Dad says with pride. "You should be able to get quite a view from your perch up there."

I'm stunned that Dad has been able to read me so well but I wish the monocular in my purse wasn't taunting me. I can almost hear it daring me to embrace the joy of the moment, to accept the gift with pure and simple gratitude, to see myself through my father's eyes. I know this is a moment I should cry but I've had a lot of practice at repressing tears, and anyway, I'd just be crying for all the wrong reasons.

"Thanks, Dad." Another two-armed hug. Two in one day. I almost lose it. Almost.

UP ON THE rooftop another surprise awaits me. An outdoor reclining chair is positioned right next to my tent, facing the city lights. I recognize it as being from that expensive home furnishing website where Marie likes to shop. A note is attached:

I hope you like it. Much love from Marie.

The truth is I love it. And yet I feel ambivalent. If it wasn't for Marie I wouldn't be living up here in the tent, and the chair makes it feel like she's okay with me being here. And even though I want Dad and Marie to be okay with me living here, I don't exactly want them to be okay with being okay. Lyla didn't get this when I explained it to her, but to me. . . well, it makes perfect sense.

So here I am and there it is. I sit down on the chair and lean back, unfolding my legs. The night is warm and the breeze feels like silk against my skin. In the distance, lights twinkle and gleam like fairy dust. I can hear the soft but deep hoot of the great-horned owl.

It's time for the hunt, my friend.

Car headlights brighten the street in front of my house and then go dark. A car door opens and shuts. When my cell phone rings I know it's either Lyla or my dad using our 'intercom' system. But it's Marie, and her voice is flush with excitement.

"Krista, are you decent? A young man is looking for you, and I'm sending him up!"

A young man? Coming up here? Why would Marie send someone up without asking me first? I suppose she's thrilled at the prospect of my having a life, which would make her attempt at having a life with Dad so much easier.

But only a few minutes later a head appears over the edge of the roof. It's Jake Robbins. He climbs the rest of the way up the ladder and then sort of does a sweep of my rooftop refuge with his eyes while my heart sets a speed record inside my chest. Once he's sized up everything, he walks over to where I'm pretending to relax on my new reclining chair. He faces me directly and looks straight into my eyes.

"Why did you do that today?" he asks.

"How did you know where I live?" I can't answer his question.

"School directory. I know who you are."

That makes sense. I knew who he was but I'm still surprised that he would be aware of me. I thought I was pretty much invisible to guys like him.

"So why'd you do it?" He's not going to give up. "Look at your house. Look at all . . . this . . ." he waves his arm in a sweeping gesture. "Your family obviously has bucks."

"I'm sorry." I can't think of any other appropriate response, and the truth is I'm not sure myself why I did it. Except for the feeling. I did it for the feeling.

"Sorry?" His voice rises in anger. "I could've lost my job if anyone knew I let you go. I gave you the chance to put it back. And you went right ahead and did it anyway!"

"So why didn't you turn me in?" It feels like he's arrived with a warrant for my arrest. I half expect him to pull out a pair of handcuffs.

"I don't know. I felt sorry for you. Everyone knows what happened . . ."

"Oh yeah, I guess I knew that. Everyone feels sorry for me." That's why I couldn't make new friends even if I wanted to. Nobody wants to be friends with someone they feel sorry for. Lyla's different. She was with me before. She knows who I really am . . . or maybe she just knows who I really was. "Well . . . thanks. Anyway, I threw it away when I got home so don't worry that I'm keeping it."

"Threw it away? That's supposed to make it all better?"

"So that's why you're here? To make everything better?"

Or is he here to make me feel worse? He's already accomplished that so I don't know what else to say. He stares at the city lights and then looks over at my tent as if seeing it for the first time.

"Why do you live in a tent on your roof?" he asks.

I shrug my shoulders. "I dunno. It's peaceful, I guess."

"Odd," he says. "Well . . . whatever." He walks back to the ladder and disappears under the lip of the roof.

What is it about Jake Robbins that succeeds in undermining my steely resolve in a way that my father and I failed to do? A few tears escape from my eyes and slide down my cheeks. I can taste their bitter saltiness on the corners of my lips. I think about the monocular that I wrapped in a bag so no one would see it in the garbage container. I thought somehow I was doing a noble thing by tossing it. Now I realize I was just taking the easy way out.

I ONCE WATCHED an entire movie without any sound. We were flying home from our vacation in Florida where we'd gone so my grandparents could have time with their grandkids. I was probably about nine years old, and my family was fast asleep in the seats next to me by the time the movie started. I didn't have a headphone set and was too shy to ask the flight attendant for one, so when the movie came on, I watched it anyway. The characters laughed. The characters cried. I could generally figure out the storyline. Still, it barely had any impact on me by the time it was over.

Years later, I saw the same movie again when it played on TV. This time I could hear what the characters said to each other, and the music soundtrack amplified each emotion. There were no awkward pauses or wasted words. It drew me in and steered me toward the powerfully moving conclusion.

Afterward, I thought about it and realized that life is more like a silent movie. If you watch a person's life unfold, you can observe her day-to-day activities. You might witness her tragedy or observe her success but you would never know the truth of what she feels inside. You couldn't hear her laughter or see her tears behind closed doors. She might be hiding a million things. Because life just goes on and on, you won't ever have a chance to see a conclusion with a clear message. And there's never any sad music that will let you know when it's time to cry.

THE NEXT MORNING, the sound of the garbage truck wakes me and I feel anxious. I know there's something that needs my immediate attention but for a few seconds I can't remember what it is. And then . . . *oh crap, the monocular!*

I pull on a pair of sweat shorts and a t-shirt and descend the ladder as quickly as I know is safe. I've been up and down this ladder so many times I have a pretty good feeling for how fast I can push it. Barefoot, I run up the driveway to the street just as the garbage truck has stopped in front of our house. The huge pincers are lowered and aimed right at the blue can containing the nonrecyclables.

"Wait!" I call out to the driver. I wave both arms over my head in the universal sign of stop-whatever-you're-doing, just in case he can't hear me above the noise of the truck. The pincers freeze mid-air. "Thanks. I lost something."

In a supremely embarrassing moment, I dig through the trash looking for the brown paper bag where I stuffed the monocular. I'm so relieved to find it that I'm almost happy. I smile and wave at the driver and he waves back with a puzzled look on his face. But now that I've salvaged the monocular, I'm not sure what to do next.

Jake said he felt sorry for me. That all the kids knew what happened. But he didn't treat me like the other kids who speak to me as though I'm made of glass—the pathetic girl who stands apart because of the horrible thing that happened in her life. Even the teachers are different with me. I get allowances that others don't when my homework is late. I get a lot of extra attention if I ask a question or need some help. But that's not what I want. I only want to be like everyone else, and yet I'm not like everyone else. Jake spoke to me as though I was a regular person . . . a bad person, maybe, but someone who could withstand normal human interaction. It felt good to be the object of his anger. I'm grateful to him.

I go in the house and text my dad:

I think I'll skip Disneyland. I'm going to hang out with friends this weekend.

That will make him happy. And it's also a lie he might have trouble believing as much as he'd love for it to be true. We both know that Lyla is my only friend and she's gone, but Dad will probably let it go. I don't think he wants to deal with Marie's two young kids and his downer daughter for the whole weekend.

I hear Charlie squawking, and I grab a carrot from the refrigerator before heading into the study. Sunlight is shining on his cage, but it's still covered with the black felt night cover. Dad and Marie must have been running late this morning and forgotten to uncover him. I can hear Charlie rustling around, wide awake but helpless to do anything about the black gloom that surrounds him. I lift the cloth, and he climbs from the floor of the cage to his perch, pulling himself up by his beak.

"Hi, Charlie boy. Sorry we forgot about you this morning," I say. He looks indignant and turns away from my apology. "I brought you a treat." I can see his tiny heartbeat beneath the pink skin of his chest. I lift the cage door and put my hand in with my finger extended out toward him. That was the signal my mom used when she wanted Charlie to come out of his cage and play. My mother could do that. She could coax any of us out of a bad state of mind—a scraped knee, a teasing at school, a tiring day at work, a scary dream, a low grade on your test. You always felt safe with Mom because you knew there was never an end to her love.

But Charlie just looks at my finger and turns away. When I don't move my hand, he gives me a gentle peck to let me know he's had enough of me. I lay the carrot on the bottom and close the door of the cage.

Chapter | 5

Rachel Sullivan is wearing a yellow sundress when she opens the door. She seems happy and surprised to see me. Rachel was Mom's best friend, but we haven't talked much since Marie moved in. I feel both relieved to finally be here and ashamed of how long it's taken. It feels like coming home in a dream— you know you're there, but everything's just a little different. Like someone came in the middle of the night while you were sleeping and moved all the furniture around.

She invites me in to see the baby as I knew she would. She mentions babysitting in the future as I also knew she would. She says the baby is sleeping in his bassinet in their master bedroom. We tiptoe to his side so as not to wake him but he's already awake. His blue-gray eyes are wide and slanted, giving him a wise and other-worldly appearance. Tufts of fine black hair sprout from his scalp. His tiny pink lips seem to be turned up in a smile but I can't be sure. It feels like he

40

knows more about me than I know about him.

"His name is Henry," Rachel offers. "Do you want to hold him?" But I don't want to. I just want to look at him right now. He's too new.

"Maybe next time," I say, hoping that Rachel won't take offense. She lets it go. I wonder if she was afraid to hold him the first time she saw him too.

Rachel picks Henry up from his bassinet and motions for us to go out to the living room.

"Can I get you something to eat or drink?" she asks.

"No, that's okay. I just wanted to come over and see you . . . and the baby." I feel a little awkward. Rachel was a person I felt totally comfortable with when my mom was alive. Now I feel a little shy around her and I don't know why. Maybe I sense that her life has become all about Henry.

"How have you been, Krista?" she asks with that special tone that everyone uses when they ask me this question.

"I've been great. Really enjoying the summer." The words sound unconvincing, even to me. Rachel is holding Henry up against her chest. She pats him lightly on his back.

"Is that really true?" She arches her eyebrows.

"Yes . . . really. I'm doing fine."

But I'm not. My eyes silently plead with her to see through the deceit of my words. So why can't I just say it?

"The last time I talked to your father he mentioned that you were seeing a therapist. Are you still doing that?"

I squirm in my seat. Maybe it was a mistake to

come here today. "No, I'm better off just talking things over with my dad."

I think of the unanswered voice messages left on the home phone as recently as last week . . .

"This is Dr. Bronstein. I'm keeping the Tuesday at five slot open for Krista whenever she decides to come back. I believe it's important for us to continue therapy. Please call."

I had pressed *delete* and wondered how many unanswered voicemails he'd leave before he called Dad at his office. Or would he give up and eventually forget? Like everyone else.

"Your dad?" she asks surprised.

"We're pretty close and we work things out together. So I'm doing great and it's better this way." *Who am I kidding? Rachel knows Dad.*

"Krista, you've been through a lot. No one would judge you for getting a little extra help. And I want you to know I'm always around if you need to talk."

Rachel *was* always around and, in the beginning, she kind of nudged me through life. Reminding me to breathe. Reminding me to live. And all the while she was navigating through the long legal process of adoption, I never stopped to consider that Rachel might have needed some nudging herself without her best friend by her side. But the more we saw of Marie, the less we saw of Rachel. I haven't seen her at all for six weeks except to wave at her when she drives by. And now there's Henry and nothing is the same.

"I still see Marie's car," she continues. "How are you two getting along?" Rachel knows how we're getting along—she can see my red tent on the roof.

"Just fine," I lie again. "She's really nice. By the way, my grandpa's coming to visit next week and he'll be staying with us." I'm relieved to have something to talk about that I know will distract Rachel from her current line of questioning.

"That's wonderful, Krista! It'll be great for you to spend some time with him. This is your mom's father right? I seem to remember your dad's father passed away."

"That's right," I say. "We have a lot of things planned. He'll be around for a while."

"I remember him from your mother's funeral," Rachel says. "I'd love to see him again if you both want to drop by for lunch one day."

"He'd probably like that." I'm suddenly anxious to leave, and I know I won't be calling her or returning anytime soon. "It's been nice seeing you and meeting Henry." I give Henry an affectionate pat. His head bobbles on top of his scrawny neck, and Rachel steadies it with her free hand. Trying to avoid squishing Henry, I give Rachel a careful hug, and she returns it with her free arm.

"Oh, Krista, please come back soon." Tears are welling up in her eyes. "I've missed you so much, and I just wish . . ." she trails off. I would give anything to trade places with Henry right now. To be held in strong, protective arms. To be caressed and loved. To be the center of someone's universe. To not even know what kind of heartache exists beyond the walls of home.

Chapter | 6

I thought of every possible excuse to not be here right now. But it seems there's no other place I can be. Doing the right thing can't be any worse than doing the wrong thing. And, in a way, I want to see if it might be better. Maybe I also want to see Jake again. Maybe I want to know what it would feel like to be seen by him as someone courageous and honorable, not as the girl who only deserves his pity and scorn. I know it's a little late for that, but I'll do my best. So that's why I'm standing in front of the store where he works with the monocular wrapped in a brown paper bag in my purse.

When I walk in, I immediately see Jake in the shoe department. In his hands, he carries a tower of shoe boxes that looks like it's being kept from falling over by invisible forces. An elderly woman in a shocking pink track suit waits for him. She has a determined look on her face that hints she might be here for a while. I walk over to the place where Jake has set the boxes down on the floor. He looks up at me from his kneeling position by the woman's feet. She pulls a crew sock over one twisted foot. The toes of her exposed foot are warped by time. Her toenails are thick and yellow.

"Can you tell me where I can find the manager?" I ask him.

Jake raises his chin in the direction of a pot-bellied, balding man in a tight green polo shirt. The man is standing behind the counter where fishing equipment is sold.

"Over there," he says. "His name is Chuck—Mr. Latham." As many times as I've seen Jake at school it feels like I'm seeing him now for the first time. He's gorgeous, although there's nothing specific that makes him that way. It's the combination of all his physical attributes and something else. His confidence. He seems to be completely comfortable being Jake Robbins.

"Thanks." I walk over to the counter.

"Something I can help you with, young lady?" the manager asks. "You interested in buying a rod and reel today?" He chuckles.

"Are you the manager?"

"That's me!" He is proud but wary. Most people who ask if he's the manager are probably about to present him with a problem. "What can I help you with?"

Suddenly I'm speechless even though I practiced this in the car on the drive over here. But soon I regain my composure, because nothing spooks me these days.

"I accidentally took this the other day." I pull the monocular from the paper bag. He looks at me skeptically. "What I mean to say is . . . I stole this from your store, and I want to return it. I'm sorry." I look him directly in the eye, and he looks away for an instant as if to spare me from my shame.

"I appreciate your honesty," he says after a moment. "What do you think I should do with you?"

His question surprises me, because I didn't think I would have a say. I know I *should* be punished for what I did, but I'm not sure what I expected—maybe jail? It's why I'm here, after all.

"Do whatever you like." I try to sound more humble than defiant. "I'm ready to accept my punishment."

"Hmm." He seems amused. "Your punishment, huh? Listen, between you and me: it's more trouble to report you than it's worth." He looks me up and down. "You seem like a nice kid, so why'd you do it?"

"I don't know." My back feels hot, and I wonder if Jake's eyes are on me.

"Well that's not helpful. I don't suppose you'd like to clean our toilets as penance?"

I must look shocked because he laughs and brings a stubby finger up to take a swipe at his nostril where thick black hairs protrude. "I can't really make you do anything without putting you on the payroll—and I'm not about to do that. I'll tell you what I'm going to do." He pauses for emphasis. "I know this was hard for you, and hopefully you've learned your lesson, so I'm gonna let you go. Now get outta here." He's pleased with himself, I can tell. He feels good about giving me a second chance but I'm surprisingly disappointed. This was not what I expected. "And next time bring your wallet," he adds.

I turn my head slightly so I can see Jake still kneeling at the feet of the woman across the store. He's looking over at me and I catch his eye but make no sign of recognition. The manager is waiting for my response to wrap this up so he can go on with his day.

"Thank you, then." I can't think of a more appropriate or grateful reply. I've done what I came to do so I head for the door. Jake's using a shoe horn to guide a sneaker onto the woman's foot—the crossfit style that cheerleaders wear at our school. She grimaces as Jake looks up at me and winks.

I'm as excited as a five-year-old girl on Christmas day.

JAKE'S FACE HAS taken up all the space in my visual memory as I play and replay his wink on a mental loop. What did it mean? Surely, it was nothing more than a silent signal of his approval, but it still feels good. And knowing that I'll have the house to myself this weekend puts me in a better than average mood. I'm even thinking of coming inside to sleep in my room while Dad and Marie are gone, but then my brief flirtation with happiness ends when I come home and Dad texts me:

> Home by 6:00. Can you pick up something for dinner? Marie isn't feeling well so we canceled D-land. Do you think you can help out with the kids this weekend?

Ugh.

Dad and Marie come home, and Marie goes right to bed without even asking about dinner. Dad and I sit together at the kitchen table and eat the Chinese take-out I picked up earlier.

He's preoccupied, which isn't unusual after a day at work. When he gets like this, I know I'm supposed to give him his space. I know from past experience if I bring up something right now, something that requires more than a few-word answer, I'll regret it. But when it's me who wants space, he pushes me to open up. He can't stand not knowing what I'm thinking.

This could be a rare moment for us to talk when Marie isn't around. It doesn't happen that often anymore, and there's stuff I want to talk about. Not the things she decides are important . . . maybe some things *I* happen to think are important. Like why is it that Marie, whom he sees all day at work, gets priority over all the other people in his life? Starting with me . . . and the Sullivans.

I take a deep breath and break the silence, not knowing how my father will react to what I'm about to say. "I went to see the Sullivans' new baby today." I've got his attention.

"Is that so?" He spreads a thin layer of hoisin sauce onto a moo shu pancake and dials down the interest in his voice. "I've heard the baby crying. Did you get to meet him?"

"Yeah, he's really cute. His name is Henry. Rachel seems happy." Dad seems to ponder this but doesn't say anything, so I go on.

"Why don't you ever go see the Sullivans anymore?" I know that Marie is the answer to this question, but I feel a devil inside of me. That's part of Dad's old life— his wife's best friend. For that matter, I'm part of Dad's old life too, but there's not much to be done about me. In a year, I'll be away at college. I wonder if one of

Marie's kids will simply take over my room. My life.

"I saw her just a few days ago," he says. "We were both out getting our newspapers, and we chatted for a while."

"That's not what I mean." Am I talking about the Sullivans, or am I talking about myself? "We used to get together a lot. Why don't we ever do that anymore?"

"We'll do that, I promise. Give Marie a chance to settle in, it's only been six weeks. Then we'll have them over."

He's answered my question but I'm seething inside. Why does everything have to be about Marie? What about me and Dad and the Sullivans?

"When things get back to normal." He adds for emphasis while bringing a napkin to his face to dab away some sauce on his chin.

But I know things will never get back to normal. Not the normal I want.

Chapter | 7

Nature's air conditioning has once again returned to the San Francisco Bay Area. That's what people here call the fog, and that's why we don't have the hot, sleepless nights in the summer that the rest of the country suffers through. From my reclining chair, I look toward the west where the sun has already disappeared behind a huge bank of fog. From here it looks like the impenetrable wall of a medieval fortress. Although the sky is clear above me and I'm comfortable in a light t-shirt and shorts, I know that behind the fog wall people are bundled up in sweaters while they walk briskly down sidewalks bathed in cool, gray mist.

I hear the rattle of the aluminum ladder and look over just in time to see Jake's head pop up over the edge of the roof.

"Knock, knock," he says. "I didn't see a doorbell, so I hope it's okay."

"Oh!" I rise from my chair. "Come on up." It seems

impossible that he's come here again even though I've wished for it a thousand times. He climbs the rest of the way and walks over to my tent.

"You know, I thought this was a strange set-up the last time I was here. But now that I'm seeing it again, it's actually pretty cool." He looks westward toward the fog bank. "Great view."

"Yeah, it's perfect. Well, it is for me, anyway. I don't have to worry about snakes or raccoons up here—only me and the owls." Gliding on rubbery wings, little, brown bats sail in and out of the branches of a gnarled oak tree.

"Only you and the owls," he repeats. "I talked to Mr. Latham after you left." He's still looking westward even though we're standing side by side. An almost perfectly formed full moon is now visible in the indigo sky. "He told me what happened. I guess you didn't mention that you knew me."

"I didn't think you'd want me to."

But I *don't* really know him, even though he doesn't feel like a stranger standing next to me. I think he's a person comfortable with whomever he's with, whether it's an old lady with painful feet, or even me. I'm close enough to smell him and it's intoxicating. He smells like a puppy or a lazy day on a sunny beach. He smells like happiness and I feel some of it siphon off into me. I've never stood next to a boy who has affected me this way. Lyla would be perfectly at ease and would know what to say. Me? I'm lost.

"What are you doing this summer?" He turns his gaze toward me now and looks in my eyes. I'm suddenly embarrassed to admit anything close to the truth. I've seen how hard he works and I don't want to lose his respect just after gaining a little of it back.

"I'm taking care of my grandpa," I say. Technically, it's the truth. "He's sick and he needs someone to drive him around and take him places."

"Do you ever get any time off?" he asks.

"Umm . . . yeah, I can arrange it when I need time off." I have no idea what my schedule will be like when my grandpa comes next week, but I can't imagine he'll demand all my time 24/7.

"I was just wondering . . . there's a summer solstice festival in Napa this weekend. Anyway, it's just a street fair, but it's kind of fun. You wanna go tomorrow night? We could eat dinner and hang out."

Eat dinner? Hang out? Could it really be that simple? In spite of Lyla's dating stories and coaching, I went from being a shy young girl to a shy older girl. In the last two years while everyone else forged ahead learning all the rules of dating life, I got left even further behind than I already was.

"How would we get there?" I ask stupidly.

"I could pick you up and drive there." He seems amused. "If it's okay with your dad."

I know this is one of those now or never decisions. I'm scared to let him into my life but I'm more scared of losing him. "My dad will be fine with it," I say quickly. "What time should I be ready?"

We make plans to meet up tomorrow afternoon. In my mind, I'm already planning how to do my hair and what clothes to wear. Do boys plan these things? It doesn't seem like Jake has this on his mind. He's talking about his job and colleges and a show about zombies that he watches on TV. He's talking about our high school principal and how the rumor is he's dating the girls' cross country coach. He's talking about surfing in Santa Cruz, and do I surf or have I ever? Would I like to learn one day?

I must seem distracted to him. I'm trying to pay attention, but I'm thinking of breaking the news to my dad that I'm driving to Napa with Jake Robbins. I'm thinking about what kind of car he'll be driving and how close I'll be sitting to him when we drive there. I'm wondering how I can manage an entire evening of conversation and still be interesting enough to hold his attention for a possible future date. I'm such a mess. By the time Jake leaves, I know I'm in for a sleepless night, and I'm already doubting the wisdom of the whole idea.

Chapter | 8

Last night when I wanted to call Lyla, I knew it would be too late for her. And now I'm afraid it will be too early. It's already Friday and a pressure behind my eyeballs has paralyzed me into inaction. It's true I didn't sleep much last night—it wasn't until daybreak that I managed to drift off, and then only for a few hours. But now it's already noon and the day is so hot that the normally golden hills seem to be pulsating white.

All morning I've thought about 758 and the brown car in the driveway with the silver paint that shows through. *Is it his car? Is he there right now?* I want to go see for myself but that pressure—just verging on a headache. All it would take is just a little nudge to send me spiraling into major headache territory and that would be the end of my night out with Jake.

Jake. Is it possible to be living a dream and a nightmare at the same time? On the dream side is Jake, of course. On the nightmare side is Jake also. How did I think this could possibly work out? I don't have a clue what I'm doing and as soon as he figures that out, he'll be kicking himself for ever asking me out in the first place. And then there's that disturbing thought in the back of my head where pressure is pushing up against my eyeballs—is this a pity date or maybe just a date to reward me for my good behavior? And how can I even think about happiness and dating when she'll never have that chance?

But if I'm not going to cancel—which I know I'm not—then I'd better get busy transforming myself into the kind of girl Jake would be seen with. Lyla can't help me so I'll have to manage on my own, learn from the mistakes I made the last time I tried to do my hair.

There's also the touchy subject of letting Dad know what I'm doing. Driving with a boy to Napa. My social life isn't an issue he's ever had to deal with before so I'm not sure how he'll react. For a moment, I consider lying and telling him I'm going to the movies with Sissy and Grace, but then I think about Jake and he doesn't seem like the kind of person who would knowingly go along with a lie. It would probably spoil the mood of the evening for me anyway if I had to worry about getting caught. I decide to tell Dad the truth and to be prepared to fight for it. If he says no, then it's probably just as well.

I call Dad at the office and, even though it's lunchtime, he's with a patient. They've been running late all morning, Marie tells me. Dad had an emergency early on and had to run over to the hospital. Ever since then they've been playing catch-up with their schedule. I remember that Marie was sick last night and ask how she's feeling.

"Decent," she says. "But not great. Alice called in sick so I had to come in to cover for her." Alice is my father's nurse. "I hope the whole staff isn't going to come down with this . . . whatever it is."

I see an opening and decide to take it. Marie was excited the first time Jake came over. Maybe she's still not too old to identify with being consumed by thoughts of a guy who takes your breath away, although I can't go to the place where that guy is my father. Maybe, as I suspected before, she just wants me to have a life so she and my dad can get on with theirs. Or maybe she's not immune to Jake's charms—I can't imagine a person who could be. Anyway, I'm pretty sure she'll be excited at the prospect of my having a date. She'll be unlikely to challenge me on it so I decide to enlist her as an ally. Jake might be the very first thing Marie and I agree on.

"Do you remember that guy who came over the other night—Jake?" I put on my most disinterested voice as though a visit from a boy was routine for me.

"Yes." Marie's voice goes up a few notches. I can feel her anticipation for what will come next.

"He wants me to go to a street fair with him tonight so I was wondering if you could just let Dad know since I'll probably be gone by the time you guys get home." I leave out the part about the street fair being in Napa, an hour's drive away.

"That's wonderful, Krista!" She's as excited as I knew she would be. "Maybe you can invite the young man in to meet us when you get home."

"Maybe. I'll see how late it is when we get back."
Not a chance, I think.

"Krista?" Marie has more on her mind and her voice is strained with sickness. "Chad and Emma are coming over tonight for the weekend. I tried to switch weekends with their father since I'm not feeling well, but he had plans he couldn't change." *Their father? Don't you mean your discarded husband . . . the one you're supposed to be with instead of my dad?* "Could you possibly go to the store to pick up a few things for the kids? I hate to ask you but by the time we get home it'll be late and I'm pretty run down as it is . . . just a few things like yogurt, milk, cereal. I can email you a list."

The pressure behind my eyes flares up. It's almost one o'clock and Jake's picking me up at four.

"I can't . . ." but then I stop myself. At least for tonight I need Marie on my side since I never got permission from my dad. "Sure, no problem." I try my best to sound upbeat.

A few things turn out to be a lot of things and by the time I've loaded up the Hornet with bags and bags of groceries it's already two-thirty. Once I'm home and the groceries are put away and the kitchen sink cleaned up, it's three. I hear Charlie squawk in the other room and go to check on him. His cage is still covered with the black felt night cloth. He's spent most of the day in the darkness, probably thinking the sun has been permanently extinguished. I rip off the cover and toss it in the corner.

"I'm so sorry Mr. Charlie!" I feel terrible. If Marie and Dad are going to neglect him, I need to make a point to check on Charlie every morning myself. His cage looks dirty, and I make a mental note to clean it tomorrow. I raise the door of his cage and extend my finger toward him. He looks away in disgust.

I'm down to forty-five minutes, which makes styling my hair an impossibility. I start to focus on a cute outfit instead. And maybe some makeup. I still need to shower and wash my hair, and I haven't even given any thought to back-up topics of conversation in case there's an awkward silence at any point. But at least I have an idea for what I'll wear. Lyla bought me a sleeveless blue silk top for my birthday last year. She claims it's my color and brings out my blue eyes. And I have a new pair of skinny jeans. Some Tory Burch ballet flats. I can pull it off—this won't be a complete disaster.

But while I'm in the shower I remember I gave my silk top to Marie to drop off at the drycleaners. Did she pick it up yet? I can't remember seeing it since then. I hurry out of the shower and look through my closet. It's not there. Then I go into the closet that used to be Mom's but is now Marie's and I look around just to be sure it didn't accidentally get mixed in with her stuff. Not there either. I run downstairs to get my new jeans. They're in the dirty laundry hamper but I can probably wear them anyway. But when I pull them out I see they're buried underneath a wet towel and have a funky odor. My options are running out one by one.

Things go from bad to worse when I realize I jumped out of the shower before conditioning my hair. Too late now. It feels frizzy and coarse and the comb catches in the tangles and pulls at my scalp. I close my eyes and press lightly against them with the tips of my fingers. Colors swirl in the black empty space of my brain but it does nothing to banish the pain. I get back to combing through the tangled mess and once I've finished, the only thing I can do is wrap my hair in a loose bun on the back of my head.

I look at my watch on the bathroom counter and it's already four o'clock. No time for makeup. The doorbell rings. I pull on an old pair of jeans and a clean, blue t-shirt. I slip on some flip-flops before I run down the stairs. Well, at least the t-shirt is blue. *Maybe it will still show off my eyes,* I think somewhat morosely. Lyla would definitely not approve.

But when I open the door Jake is smiling, and barely-there dimples adorn his face. His jeans are faded and he wears a water-polo team t-shirt that looks like it's had multiple encounters with a washing machine.

"You look pretty," he says. We match each other perfectly. Suddenly, I'm grateful for the wet towel on my skinny jeans and the missing silk top . . . and the pain in my head has simply disappeared.

Chapter | 9

Jake drives a Jeep with bucket seats in the front, so it's clear where I'm supposed to sit—in my own seat. I don't know what I was expecting, since most cars have front bucket seats, but last year Lyla dated a guy who drove a truck with a bench seat. She would sit in the middle right next to him, or anyway that's what she told me. I'm glad that wasn't a choice I had to make. *I can't believe I'm actually going on a date with a boy—my first. And Jake Robbins!* I'm relieved I didn't reach Lyla after all. There's less pressure if I just tell her about everything after it's over.

One thing I don't have to worry about is how to make conversation. Jake is easy to be with, and now that I'm not obsessing over what to do with my hair or how to break the news to my dad, I can focus on what he's saying. So we just talk about school, friends, and our favorite vacations. Jake tells me that my father is his next-door neighbor's doctor, but when I don't respond he drops it and doesn't bring up my family or my personal life anymore, which I appreciate.

"Should I turn on some music?" he asks.

But I don't want to listen to music right now. I just want to listen to his voice. "Maybe on the way back," I suggest.

We're on a two-lane highway lined by miles of vineyards. When I look out the window it's just a blur of jade-green leaves, each vine reaching out to join with its neighbor. I see a huge jackrabbit hopping between the rows, and Jake slows down so I can get a better look at it. I've never seen a rabbit this big before. It keeps running and looks slightly panicked. I half expect it to pull out a pocket watch and announce that it's late for an important date.

"Do you want to know something funny?" Jake asks and the corner of his mouth turns up in an irresistible half-smile.

"What?"

"When we were in the seventh grade I had a crush on you."

I think I detect a slight shift in the color of his face—a pinkening that wasn't there before but he looks straight ahead and I can't be sure.

"No way! I didn't even know you. I mean . . . I don't even really know you now."

"Nah, but . . . okay, I already stuck my foot in it so why stop now? My buddies and I sat at the table in the cafeteria right across from where you used to sit sometimes. With your friend . . . Lyla? And I used to position myself so I could watch you eating. Creepy, huh?"

"But . . ." Now it's my turn to flush pink, and I'm sure it's happening from the flash of heat that explodes in my face. "No . . . you're just saying . . . no, it's not creepy at all."

The heat in my face slides down into my heart.

"Okay, now that that embarrassing moment is over. . ."

"Lyla's gone for the summer," I say. It seems vital for me to shift away from this moment of intimacy. Intimacy is something that still feels strange to me—like a language I used to speak but have now forgotten.

"Oh yeah? Where'd she go?"

"To see her grandparents in Maine. They have a house right on the beach."

The corner of his mouth slides up again, awakening an enchanting dimple—the one I can see with him staring straight ahead at the road.

"That must be nice," he says. "A summer with nothing to do. A house on the beach."

"You surf, right? So you must spend time at the beach too."

"Whenever I can. But it's not like living on the beach. It takes me more than an hour to get there and even then, I can only go when I'm not working at the store or helping my dad with his business."

I want to ask Jake about his job and his friends at school and the kind of work he does for his dad. I try to file these questions away for the inevitable awkward pause I'm sure is still coming.

"I can't imagine surfing here. The water's so cold."

"That's why God invented wetsuits." He laughs and I have an urge to reach out and touch his arm, the one that's carelessly draped over the steering wheel. But then I think about the house—758—and my joy suddenly seems so selfish and . . . so wrong.

We arrive at the summer solstice fair, which is about fifteen minutes past Napa. Somehow the extra distance has made me just a little more nervous and I wonder if I should have told my father where I was going. We park in an unused dirt lot that has been converted to a parking area for the weekend event. Crowds of people are already gathered, although Jake assures me it will get much busier as the night goes on. There are booths selling wine glasses engraved with *Summer Solstice 2016*. I want to buy one as a memento, and they're only ten dollars, but Jake says you have to be twenty-one because the glass is like a ticket for the night for unlimited wine tasting from the local vineyards. He tells me not to worry—he'll get me a different souvenir.

We head over to the olive oil tasting, which Jake assures me is the new happening thing to do. There are vats of olive oil flavored with lemon, with garlic, with rosemary and basil. There seem to be as many varieties of olive oil as there are varieties of wine. I fill a tiny plastic cup with extra virgin olive oil and then soak up its contents with a small chunk of sourdough bread. When I pop it in my mouth it burns the back of my throat and makes me cough.

Jake laughs. "That's a positive," he says. "Good olive oil is supposed to burn."

"How do you know so much?" I ask him.

"My parents used to bring us here every year when I was younger." He smiles. "Did you know that an olive is a fruit, not a vegetable?"

It feels good to be here with him. I'm relaxed. I'm having fun. The nerve pathways are growing back.

We walk through the huge fairgrounds, someone's cow pasture, now dry and dusty from the California summer sun. Jake buys me a mango flavored cotton candy. Then we go back for the blueberry flavor. The mayor of the town sits on a chair above a dunk tank. Jake pays for a set of three baseballs and takes aim at the lever that will send the mayor plunging into the tank. He smoothly and expertly winds up and releases the first ball, which hits its target and releases the platform that holds the mayor's chair. Everyone applauds and laughs as the mayor climbs out of the tank sputtering and smiling, readying himself for his next dunking.

"He's a good sport." Jake smiles at his success. "Not every mayor volunteers for that." He gives me the blue teddy bear he wins as a prize.

Later, we find an open picnic table and eat a dinner of locally made apricot-chicken sausage and brie cheese with sourdough bread. We gulp down red plastic cups of brown apple cider. The day has turned gold and a crazy quilt of shadows and light drapes over the vine-striped hills.

Slowly, the gold sinks from the sky and settles on the horizon. Pink pancake clouds hover above us. Jake smiles at me and I smile back at him. Does nature serve up anything more delicious than a warm summer night?

ON THE WAY home, we're both quiet so I ask Jake to turn on some music. He selects a playlist and by the songs he plays I can tell he's thoughtful and different from a lot of kids who just listen to current pop. Jake's got some jazz and other things like classic rock. It's dark now and I can't see outside my window anymore, only the lights from the occasional oncoming car. Dim at first, and then brighter and stronger until the moment they pass and then darkness returns. A song comes on that Mom used to love and for a second my heart freezes over. I want to stop the car and get out, but then I take a deep breath and keep listening. It sounds beautiful right here, right now in this car next to Jake.

> *Black sky melting in a piecrust moon*
> *Whispered promises to stay*
> *Never thought you'd be gone so soon*

I know these lyrics. I've heard them so many times before.

> *Didn't know you'd go away*

I think of the old guitar that's still in our garage. I think about Mom strumming the notes of this song and her sweet soft voice, how we all would hop on her bed to sing along. I reach over to turn off the radio.

"Tired of the music," Jake states more than asks. His voice is soft and merciful.

"I feel like talking," I answer. But the magic is gone. As soon as the hopefulness of the evening has left me, the conversation just seems like words.

When we get back it's still early. I don't have to be home until midnight and I could probably push that another thirty minutes if I text Dad first. I know that Chad and Emma will be there by now, and if they're awake it won't be easy to slip by them on my way up to the tent. Dad would consider that rude. Marie too.

And they'd want to meet Jake, so I'm not anxious for the evening to end.

Jake has a plan. During the summer, he has a side job working for the water polo coach. He does daily testing of the pool water at our high school in between the weekly visits of the pool service. He has a key to get in.

"Wanna go?" he asks. "No one's around at night and I haven't done a water test yet today."

It sounds like a reasonable plan to me. I know the pool well since my father makes me do swim team during the school year. It will be interesting to see the pool at night when no one is around.

When we get there, Jake retrieves a chemical testing kit from the boys' locker room in the gym. It's a strange experience to be in the boys' locker room. It seems forbidden—an alien environment. I can imagine the rowdiness that takes place here when school is in session but for now it's deserted. Ghosts of generations of boys roam through the halls.

We walk through the back door of the gym where Jake unlocks the gate that leads to the pool. He pulls out the testing kit and mixes some chemicals with a small sampling of pool water. He shakes the plastic vial and holds it up to the light. Apparently, it turns the proper color.

"You want to swim?" He has a mischievous look on his face.

I dip my toes into the water. It feels warm and silky. I'm sticky from the heat. Nature's air conditioning didn't arrive tonight.

"I guess so," I say. "But I don't have a suit."

"Neither do I," he says. "I'll turn off the lights."

He disappears into the gym, and when he reappears we're lit only by the full moon which now looks like one of those butterballs you put on a waffle. Jake pulls off his t-shirt and jeans and kicks off his flip-flops. The moonlight strokes the soft curves of the muscles on his chest and arms. His boxers are form fitting. He takes my breath away.

I undress down to my bra and panties and jump in quickly before he can look too closely. I can't believe that I'm doing this. My first date with a boy and I've already undressed. Jake dives in gracefully and surfaces by my side.

"Look up at the sky," he says and when I tilt my head back he lifts my legs and cradles me in his arms. A million stars look like glitter thrown against a black canvas. He rotates me three hundred and sixty degrees while I take in the celestial splendor. "It's like your own private planetarium," he says, "only better because it's real."

I wriggle out of his arms and splash him with water. "I'll race you—twenty-five yards, any stroke!"

"You're on." He pulls himself out of the water and walks to the end of the pool. "Winner gets to choose the prize."

I pull myself out of the pool and stand in the lane next to him. "Swimmers take your marks!" I do my best imitation of a swim meet announcer, but before I mimic the starting buzzer I dive in and start swimming. Jake gives me a few more seconds before diving in. By the time he surfaces, I've covered half the pool length and he's already by my side. I'm doing my best freestyle and he's doing butterfly. I can't stop laughing and I grab onto his foot to try to hold him back from the finish line. But then we reach the end and he touches the wall seconds before I do.

"And the winner is . . . me!" He laughs and holds up his fist in a victory salute. "Winner gets to choose the prize," he says again.

"Which is?"

He puts his hands behind my shoulders and pulls me to him. And then he leans over to kiss me softly on the lips. I so badly want him to kiss me, but I don't at the same time, and I'm furious with myself for my confusion. And then my anger turns on him and I push him away.

"What're you doing?" I ask indignantly.

"I'm trying to kiss you." He looks shocked. I doubt he's ever had this reaction from a girl before.

"Why?"

"Are you kidding?" He must feel like he's in the middle of a bad movie.

"No. Are *you* kidding?"

Doesn't he know who I am? Doesn't he know I'm *that* girl? The broken girl. The girl who breaks things. The one with no right to feel happiness . . . or love. I swim to the side and climb up the steps. I have a hell of a time pulling my jeans over my wet legs. Then I put on my t-shirt. Jake gets out and walks over to his pile of clothes. He uses his t-shirt to dry himself and then puts on his jeans and flip-flops.

"Let's go, I'll take you home." He sounds sad and embarrassed. I feel embarrassed and foolish. I hate myself.

THE RIDE HOME is totally silent. Jake's wet t-shirt is bunched up on the console between us. I try to avoid looking at him because I remember the effect it had on me when he first took his shirt off.

Finally, he breaks the silence. "What's wrong with you?" He sounds hurt.

"Why does something have to be wrong with *me*?" If I wanted a chance to make things better, I just blew it.

"I don't get you," he says finally.

"Well, then you're just like everyone else."

"How's that?" he asks, clearly wounded to be thought of as just like everyone else.

"Nobody gets me," I manage to say without breaking down.

When we get to my house Jake picks up his wet t-shirt and pulls it on. He walks around to my side of the car and opens the door for me. I'm screaming inside; I so desperately want to make everything right again, but I don't know what to say. We walk in silence to the front door. I'm just about to sob out an apology but the motion detector activates and all the front door lights come on.

"Thanks for the night," he says. "I'll see you around."

And then he's gone.

When I go inside the house, only Chad is awake. He's in the family room in front of the big screen TV with the volume so low I can barely hear it. He's probably watching something he's not supposed to be watching. When he hears me he quickly picks up the remote and turns off his show.

"How was your *date*?" He places a sarcastic emphasis

on the word date.

"Hi, Chad. Nice to see you too." I ignore his question. "Why are you up so late?" I open the refrigerator in the adjoining kitchen and pull out a bottle of sparkling water. Right now I don't have the patience for twelve-year-old boys who are angry at the world and therefore angry at me. Not that I blame him; in fact, I can totally relate. Chad and I are like cellmates in forced confinement. At least Marie doesn't have custody of her kids—their father made sure of that. Marie's living arrangement was the deciding factor for the family court judge. Anyway, they're not around all that much as a result.

"So, I guess Disneyland isn't happening," Chad says. "I wonder what fun things you have planned for us this weekend." The sarcasm hasn't left his voice.

"What do you mean *us?* Leave me out of it."

"Mom says you're going to do something with me and Emma tomorrow. She's not feeling well . . . remember? So what are we going to do?"

For the first time, I think about Emma. She sleeps in one of the twin beds in the guest room with Chad. The other two empty bedrooms are off limits to her even though I'm not currently using mine. Emma says the house is too big and it scares her. She says it has ghosts. Chad must have ducked out of the room once she fell asleep and sneaked downstairs to watch TV by himself.

I think about Jake, his skin wet and glistening under the moonlight. I think about being in his arms while I look up at a sky full of glittering gold. I think about drinking rich brown cider and driving down a dark and empty two-lane highway with a sad song playing in the background. I've left the blue teddy bear behind in Jake's car. Not even a souvenir to remember the night.

"Good night, Chad." I've forgotten what he just said to me. "See you tomorrow."

Chapter | 10

Every family has its own lore, which is something I learned about in Honors English last year. Each day of our lives, stories are created just by doing the things we do. As time goes by, the family comes to an unspoken agreement on what the favorite stories are going to be, and these are the ones that get repeated. As more time goes on, the stories change a little to make them more interesting. By consensus, the family usually goes along with that too.

Here's the earliest contribution I made to my own family lore. I was only three years old at the time and we were vacationing in Florida, having a day on the beach. Somehow, someone took their eye off me for a second and I melted into the crowd of sunscreened beachgoers. When Mom found me she was frantic, but I was happily digging in the sand with a broken plastic shovel that some other child had abandoned.

"You got lost," I said to her, and then went back to

my digging.

No matter who told this story it would always be followed by laughter. It was a funny thing, right? I was the one who was lost and yet I thought it was Mom. But now I can't seem to remember the girl who always thought she knew where she was.

"KRISTA!" EMMA'S AT the bottom of the ladder calling up to me. She's not allowed to climb the ladder. Neither is Chad, thank goodness for that. "Are you awake yet?"

I hear the ladder rattling violently and I know it's Chad. Emma would never be that bold.

"Knock it off!" I yell from inside the tent. "I'll be down in a while." I do a quick mental calculation. It's Saturday, so this must be the day I'm expected to pitch in with the kids who Marie rarely sees. Yes, she's sick. Yes, she runs my father's office like a well-oiled machine, as he's fond of saying.

Henry's crying has become one of the usual sounds I can now sleep through. "La la la." His puny lungs can only manage short eruptions so far. In twelve years, he could be rattling someone's ladder.

There's no going back to sleep now so I get up and throw on my sweat shorts and the blue t-shirt I wore last night. Magic happened inside that t-shirt, and this morning I still can't believe it. Now I know how Cinderella felt when her carriage turned back into a pumpkin. But it crosses my mind I won't ever get a second chance with the prince.

Emma's wearing a pair of yellow capri leggings with

a white frilly blouse. She's squatting on the driveway, being careful not to let any dirt soil her outfit. When she hears the ladder creaking she looks up with excitement in her eyes and tosses back her silvery blonde hair. She stands up and runs to the bottom of the ladder to greet me.

"Yay! What are we doing today?" she asks.

Chad is lying on his back on the driveway with his arms and legs outstretched in a snow angel position. He looks up at me and, once I've reached the bottom of the ladder, he stands too but says nothing.

"Let me get some breakfast and see what's going on." I walk into the house with the kids trailing after me.

Dad and Marie are in their bedroom with the door shut.

"Mommy's sick," Emma says forlornly.

"Your dad's sick too," Chad adds.

Freaking great. Now all that's left is for me to get sick, which seems preferable to being stuck entertaining Chad and Emma.

"So what are we going to do?" they ask, almost in unison.

"Let me think! God, I just woke up." They have no idea they're being punished for my own stupidity last night. "Go watch TV while I eat."

"Mommy says we're not supposed to watch TV," Emma says. But Chad goes over and turns on the set anyway.

"It's okay to watch because Krista gave us permission." He's smart and he's already planned his defense if Marie should catch him breaking her rules.

Emma's not having any of that. She knows that her mother's intent is more important than any technicalities. She pulls a Barbie doll out of a pink backpack that is lying on the floor and gets to work combing the doll's hair with a tiny, pink, plastic brush.

I'm beginning to feel a little guilty. "Alright, here's what we're going to do." Emma's face lights up and Chad actually turns away from his show about the world's most dangerous professions. "We're going to clean Charlie's cage." I feel somewhat proud that I've come up with this.

"That doesn't sound like fun," Chad turns back to the TV. Emma's smile falls upside down.

"Just help me do it and I'll think of something fun for later. But first help me empty the dishwasher." Emma immediately walks over and stacks dishes according to size on the counter. After a few minutes, Chad turns off the TV and begins to pull out the cutlery, handing me the spoons and forks one by one. He's slowing me down but I'm not going to let him get away with doing nothing.

When we're done with the morning dishes we carry a garbage bag and some corn cob bedding for the cage bottom into the study. Charlie squawks with interest. He doesn't usually get this many visitors.

"Ew! He's gross," Emma shrieks after one look at his featherless breast. Chad holds the leaf of lettuce I told him to select for Charlie's treat.

"Come on, Charlie boy." I stick my finger into the cage next to him but he ignores it.

"I don't think he likes you," Chad helpfully offers. Chad knows because he doesn't like me so much himself.

We pull out the perches and sand away the accumulated bird poo, and Emma trots off to the bathroom to scrub out his water dish. She returns with a fresh dish of water filled so high that it spills with every step she takes.

"What's that white stuff in the bird poo?" she asks when we empty the dirty litter into the garbage bag.

"That's bird poo too, idiot." Chad turns away from my fierce glare and carefully inserts the leaf of lettuce between two bars of Charlie's cage. "Okay, now what?" he asks.

"Do you guys want to see a movie?" I'm thinking of the theater at the mall where Jake works. I turned things around once in that sporting goods store. Maybe I can do it again.

"Yay! A movie!" Emma hops up and down.

"What movie?" Chad asks suspiciously.

"Something you both agree on. Come on, let's go check out what's playing."

"Why are we here?" Chad demands to know when we pull into the covered parking lot of the mall. "There's a theater much closer to where you live. And it's a lot nicer than this."

"This is a nice theater," I say. "C'mon, let's go." I'm anxious to get to the store where Jake works. It's a little out of the way and I don't want them to miss the beginning of the movie.

Once we get there, I can't bring myself to go in not knowing what kind of reception I'll get from Jake.

"Chad, go in and walk around and see if there's a guy working who's about my age and has wavy brown hair," I say. I've begun to feel that Chad and Emma are my captives and I can do what I want with them. This is probably why my father is so frustrated with me all the time. I've grown past the age where he can make me do things.

Chad is gone for a long time—about ten minutes. Emma starts to fret.

"Where's Chad? What if someone kidnapped him?" she wants to know. "Daddy won't let us go into a store by ourselves."

"We're standing at the door," I try to reassure her. "Nobody could take him without going past us." Nevertheless, I'm starting to feel a little worried, and I'm just about to go in when Chad strolls out.

"Did you see him?" I can't disguise the intense interest in my voice even though I try.

"Jake?" Chad asks.

"Yeah, how did you know?"

"He was wearing a name tag."

"So you saw him?" Chad's not going to tell me anything voluntarily. I'll have to pry it out of him. "Did he look like he was busy?" I'm trying to build up my nerve to go in and say hi.

"Busy with a pretty girl," Chad smirks.

"What do you mean?"

"I mean just talking to a really pretty girl, like . . . flirting, you know. She was laughing a lot." I can tell Chad is enjoying this despite the thoughtful look he's trying to wear.

"Let's go before we miss the start of the movie."

They follow me toward the theater. My cheeks are burning with shame.

THE MOVIE IS an animation about zoo animals and wild animals. It's just peaceful enough that I manage to fall asleep. When it's over Emma shakes my arm. My neck is twisted at an awkward angle and a little spit pools at the side of my mouth. Chad looks at me in disgust.

"You slept late enough today," he scolds me. "Can't you manage to stay awake during the day?"

I sit up straight and shake the fog from my brain. Chad has a point. Emma strokes my hair in the dark theater while the credits roll.

"Be nice to Krista! Maybe she's getting sick too." She's partially right. I've been sick for two years.

"Now what?" Chad wants to know.

"I don't know. What would you be doing if you were at your own house?" I can't even figure out what I want to do, let alone plan for Emma and Chad.

"Playing with friends," they say in unison and then burst out laughing.

"And swimming and going to the water park and playing video games," Chad adds.

"And I have all my stuff at my house and nothing but one Barbie here." Emma senses a grave injustice. "And we were supposed to go to Disneyland." She draws out "land" into about three syllables.

"Let's go for a drive, I'll bet you don't get to do that very often when you're at home." The lights of the theater are on and two employees roll a large garbage can through the aisles. One of them tosses empty popcorn and soda containers into it while the other sweeps under the seats.

"Yay! A drive." Emma claps her hands together and hops up and down. "Can I sit in front this time?"

"Yeah, sure. You guys take turns."

"Emma's not allowed to sit in the front," Chad says. "She's too little. Mom will get mad."

"I am too!" Her face scrunches up like she's about to cry.

"Okay, okay. How about Emma sits in front until we get where we're going and then you guys can trade again?" I hope this will put an end to the argument. I just want to get going.

Emma seems surprised but happy, like she's just pulled off a major manipulation. I worry that maybe Chad is telling the truth and not just looking for trouble. I'll make sure to drive extra safely.

"So where is it?" Chad asks.

"Where's what?"

"Where is it that we're going? You said when we get there we can switch seats."

"Oh . . . you'll see when we're there. I think you'll find it interesting."

Chad looks skeptical. I feel like a scumbag for what I'm about to do.

"Why are we driving here?" Emma is nervous.

"Obviously, this isn't a real drive," Chad says. "This is just someplace that Krista wants to go and she's making us go with her."

Emma swivels her head to look at me. She doesn't want Chad to be right but she knows he usually is.

"Don't be silly guys." I look at Chad in my rearview mirror. He's slumped in the back seat, his arms folded across his chest. "This is a sort of like a field trip. You can see how other people live. People who don't have money like us."

"We don't have a lot of money," Chad sulks. "Not like your dad."

"We're not poor like this, Chad." Emma swings around in her seat to defiantly face down her brother.

"No, not like this." Chad is slightly on the defensive and has decided it might not be such a good thing to identify with this neighborhood. "Our house is a lot nicer."

I perform a U-turn in the middle of the street and pull into my usual spot facing 758 but on the wrong side of the street. Today the driveway is empty and no one's outside.

"Why are we stopping? I'm scared." I detect a mild tremble in Emma's voice.

"Let's just sit for a while." I put on my most reassuring voice. "We're safe in the Hornet." I push the auto lock button and both doors make a clicking sound. "Just stay in the car and don't get out."

"I'm squished back here. I don't understand why we have to stay. We've seen what we came to see which is how poor people live." Chad is too big for the Hornet's back seat. I should have let him sit up front.

"Okay, hang on. You guys can switch seats in a few minutes."

The front door of 758 opens, and the boy walks out with his ball. A younger girl follows him out and sits on the dried grass of the front lawn. She's barefoot and wearing a faded pair of green shorts and a Barbie T-shirt. Emma and Chad are instantly mesmerized.

"Are those poor kids?" Emma is wide-eyed.

"Of course they are, idiot!"

I give Chad a backward angry glare in the rearview mirror. "Cool it with the negative language or I'll tell your mom."

"I'll tell my mom where you took us," Chad shoots back. I hadn't said anything about not telling their mom but they're smart kids and quickly understand this is something to be kept between the three of us. "And that you let Emma sit up front."

"Don't get Krista in trouble." Emma twists her body in order to look directly at her brother.

"Okay, okay. Everyone just settle down. Nobody's getting anybody in trouble." I put on my adult voice hoping to give them the false impression that I have everything under control.

The boy stands in the driveway and begins to juggle the ball with his right foot. He's skillful considering the lack of control one can usually exert over a ball that bouncy.

Chad watches him carefully. "He's pretty good," he says after a few minutes. "Better than anyone on my soccer team."

He seems a little older than Chad. More mature.

The ball has been kicked a little too high and it bounces into the street. It rolls almost directly in front of my car due to the slight downward angle of the road. With lightning quick speed, Emma unlocks the door and jumps out of the car to retrieve the ball.

"Emma!" Chad and I both call after her at the same

time. I get out of the car and Chad's right behind me.

But Emma has already picked up the ball. She smiles brightly at the young boy who's come to retrieve it. She pauses for a minute and then tosses it to him with perfect accuracy. The boy returns her smile and then runs back to his front lawn. His younger sister watches the scene from the safety of her front lawn. She is wide-eyed.

"Idiot!" Chad grabs Emma by the hand. "Krista said to stay in the car." His voice is mean but I know he's just feeling protective of her.

The woman, who is obviously their mother, walks out the front door and calls to them in her language. Their faces register disappointment and the boy walks into the house with his sister right behind him. Then the woman turns and looks directly at me.

"Go!" she speaks loudly in thickly accented English. "Leave the children alone! I know who you are." She turns and walks into the house, slamming the door behind her.

Chad and Emma are standing next to the Hornet with shocked expressions. I open the passenger side door.

"Get in. Let's go." I avoid eye contact with them.

"How does that lady know you, Krista?" Emma asks as she scrambles into the back seat. There's no arguing about who sits where anymore.

"Why did you get out of the car?" Chad is clearly upset and doesn't know any other way to deal with his fear. He must now make this about Emma.

Emma's face scrunches up again but this time she really does cry. A man who lives next door comes out of his house and stands on his front lawn. He looks over at the Hornet and shakes his head.

"Let's go get ice cream," I suggest. But there is no exclamation of delight or clapping of hands from Emma, and Chad merely grunts.

When we walk in the door, Marie is waiting for us. She hasn't seen the kids all day and she asks them if they've had fun. Emma runs to her mother and hugs her.

"Are you feeling better, Mommy?"

Chad wants to know if we have a soccer ball that he can borrow for a while. He goes off to the garage in search of it. My father is still in bed and has been sleeping all day.

"How was your date last night, Krista?" Marie turns her attention to me. "We tried to wait up for you last night but, honestly we were both feeling so rotten."

"It was good." I know this kind of noncommittal answer drives parents crazy, but it's the best I can come up with. "We had fun."

Where would I begin even if I did want to tell her how the date went? He's the perfect guy. He's nice. He's smart. He's interesting and seemed interested in me. It's the first time ever that a guy's asked me out on a date, and I still can't believe it was Jake Robbins. And . . . oh yeah, I managed to completely screw everything up.

"Is he a nice young man?"

"Very nice."

"Well, I'm sorry your father and I didn't get to meet him. Maybe next time." This is her way of trying to find out if there will even be a next time.

"Maybe," I say and am about to excuse myself to do

some reading in the tent when I notice that Chad's back from the garage holding a soccer ball under his arm. I'm not sure how long he's been standing there listening to me and Marie.

"What was the name of the guy you went out with last night?" he asks.

"Jake, wasn't it Krista?" Marie asks.

"Yeah . . . Jake." I flash a warning look at Chad but his eyes don't betray a thing.

Chapter | 11

The shadow of the oak is over my tent, and it's starting to cool down, so I go straight to the lounge chair. I pick up *The Great Gatsby* which is one of the books I'm supposed to read before school starts but the words make about as much sense to me right now as a column of marching ants. I'm worried about Chad and Emma. I shouldn't have taken them with me, especially Emma who's too young to understand and too old not to notice. I guess I shouldn't have let her ride in the front seat either. Chad now has loads of ammunition he can use against me if he wants and I'm not sure how much I can trust him. And I can't get the woman's awful words out of my head.

Chad has brought the soccer ball outside. I hear it bouncing on the driveway and it makes me think of the boy at 758. I walk to the edge of the roof and look down. Chad's practicing his juggling skills with a fierce look of determination on his face. My stomach feels hollow, and for the first time, I consider it might be from hunger instead of nerves. Marie was still in her pajamas and my dad is asleep so if I'm going to eat I need to figure something out myself.

I hear my phone chime and walk back to the lounge chair to see who's texting me. It's a message from Lyla with a tiny image I click on to enlarge. Two petite and perfectly formed feet—toenails shining with bright orange polish—centered in a grassy green frame. At the top of the image, ocean wavelets twinkle under a setting sun.

Wish you were here.

I wish I was there too. Lyla would know exactly what to do about Jake, even though I don't think I could bear to face him and I'm sure he has no interest in seeing me again. It occurs to me she might not even believe me if I told her we went out on a date. It sounds crazy even to me. I know Lyla would help keep me out of trouble too. My track record isn't great so far and there's still a long summer ahead. With Lyla there'd be someplace to go right now and something to do.

Still, there is 758, and I know I can't stay away. Why should I? Life isn't fair, so why do I have to be the one to move along and pretend like nothing ever happened? But now I know it's something I have to do by myself. Lyla can't make it easier, and Emma and Chad can't either. I don't know what I was thinking when I took them along.

I hear a bounce when the ball hits the pavement followed by a series of lesser bounces and then silence. It's a sign that Chad has failed to keep the ball in the air, but from the soft thumps that soon follow I can tell he keeps trying.

My grandfather is coming on Tuesday, and then I'll have my purpose, at least for a while. In a strange way, I'm looking forward to it. Being in the house with us he'll be able to understand in a way others can't. Marie is in his dead daughter's bed. Her clothes fill my mother's empty closet. Her voice presides over dinners that were once our family's special time. Her hand never caresses the curve of my cheek. Her lips never touch the top of my head just before I climb into bed. Her questions, although friendly enough, never reach deep into the part that's really me.

How could Grandpa not be affected? It's not exactly like I want someone on my side . . . it's just that I want someone who can feel what I'm feeling. And miss what I'm missing. Someone who will instantly notice the gaps in my life. The empty places that used to be full. Dad used to understand. Grandpa will, I'm sure.

When my mother was alive she kept notes about her father's experiences in World War II Hungary. I know because I found them one day when Dad was cleaning out Mom's closet in preparation for Marie's arrival. They were handwritten into a journal and were in a box marked for the garage. I read through them that day and was surprised at the absence of emotion and pain. There were facts and even details, but nothing that matched the power of the word scrawled in black marker across the cover—HOLOCAUST.

Once I walked in on my mother when she was filming an interview with her father about this time in his life. He chose his answers carefully, in a way that was polite but distant—informative without really saying anything. Eventually, my grandmother walked into the room and stood behind him. With her lips pursed together, she shook her head at my mother and waved her hands in a sign to put an end to the questioning. She was trying to protect him. My mother turned the camera off and the questions came to an end. I was young and not terribly interested in something an old man with a thick accent had to say.

When I can't hear the ball bouncing anymore, I look over the edge of the roof. Chad is sitting on the driveway, leaning against the wall with the ball in his lap.

"What's for dinner?" He looks up at me. "I'm hungry."

"What did your mom say?"

"She said that maybe we could go pick up some dinner and bring something back for Emma too. Your dad and my mom don't want anything."

"Emma can come with us."

"She doesn't want to," Chad says in a way that lets me know it's already been offered and refused. The way his eyes cast downward makes me wonder if I'm poison to her now.

"You wanna come with me to pick up Chinese?"

"I can help pay," he says. "I just got my allowance."

"That's alright. I have my own credit card that my dad pays for." I'm actually beginning to feel sorry for this kid.

He follows me into the Hornet. Neither of us makes any mention of the day's events although there's plenty to talk about. We've somehow arrived at a truce—or maybe an understanding.

When we get home and walk through the door, it's obvious to me that a black gloom has settled over the house just like the black, felt cloth that covers Charlie's cage at night. Dad has gotten out of bed and he doesn't look well. He's sitting at the kitchen table with Marie who avoids looking up at me. Emma is also in the kitchen, but she leaves as soon as Chad and I walk in.

"We brought dinner, Emma," I call after her.

"Krista, can I have a word with you?" Dad ignores the food that I set down. "In my bedroom, now, please." Chad looks from my father to me.

Dad gets up from the kitchen table with effort, and I follow him into his room, closing the door behind me as I've been trained to do when we have our private talks. The bed is a mess with sheets rumpled into balls and covers thrown off onto the floor. The blinds are still drawn. It has the look and feel of a room where people suffer from illness. The musty smell of fever.

"Where were you today, Krista?" He turns to me with glassy eyes.

"I took the kids to a movie. Then we went for ice cream." I'm scrambling.

"Please don't disrespect our relationship, Krista. I need the truth from you." He looks pained.

"We went for a drive," I add. How much more do I need to give him? What does he know? "And we stopped at a sporting goods store for a few minutes."

"A drive where?" he asks. Apparently, the sporting goods store is of no interest to him.

"I wanted to show them how poor people—"

"—Think about what you're going to say," he cuts me off. "Don't commit yourself to a lie."

"If you already know what I did, then why are you asking me?" I realize that Emma must have folded. That's why she fled when she saw me. But I don't blame her. She's just a baby and she had a scare today. I blame myself . . . but I don't blame myself . . .

"What on earth do you think you're doing, Krista? Taking the children to that place. Why are *you* even going there—subjecting yourself to that? You need to go back to Dr. Bronstein. If you're not going to talk to me then I'm going to insist that you get professional help."

"I don't *want* professional help and I don't *need* professional help." The volume of my voice rises along with the pitch. "Why do you think I need help any more than you do?"

"I'm not behaving in an irresponsible and reckless manner, Krista. I'm not lying around the house moping all day. I'm moving on with my life."

"Yeah, right. You're moving on with your life. I guess I noticed that." There's so much I could say to him right now that would be supremely hurtful. I've gone over these things so many times in my head that it would be easy just to open the floodgates and let the words spill out. But somehow I manage to control it. I know that whatever I say right now, I'll probably regret tomorrow. So I turn around and walk out of the room, slamming the door behind me.

"Krista," Chad has heard the door slam. He's been waiting for me.

"Not now," I walk to the front door.

"Aren't you going to have dinner with us?" he asks. He looks hurt . . . and scared. He's no stranger to family drama and this can't be pleasant for him.

"No, not tonight." I head straight for the Hornet and the peace and solitude of a directionless drive.

WHEN I WAS in fourth grade I had trouble sleeping at night. I was convinced my teacher didn't like me, and there were a few girls who had invited Lyla but not me to sleepovers and birthday parties, so I thought my best friend was being taken away from me. It all seems silly when I look back on it now, but it was so serious at the time. Whenever I'd go to bed, my thoughts would turn dark, and soon I convinced myself that I would never be able to sleep again.

It was during this time that Mom would bundle me up in a blanket and strap me into the backseat of the car as if I was a baby. She'd drive through the hills with the moonlight streaming through the windows and soft classical music playing on the car's stereo. I'd look out at the twisted tree branches silhouetted against the moon and I'd imagine I was on an African safari with elephants and lions lurking just beyond the shadows. By the time my mother pulled up in the driveway of our house, I would be sound asleep. My father would lift me from the car and carry me to my bed.

One day I realized I no longer had trouble sleeping and the night rides came to an end. But I missed those times when it was just me and Mom, so some nights I'd pretend to be all wound up—and I think she pretended to believe me because she might have missed them too.

ALTHOUGH I LEFT my house with no destination in mind, I know there's no such thing as a direction-less drive. Everyone always knows where they're going, even if they don't admit it to themselves. So I find myself driving down a cozy street in a neighborhood some miles away from mine. The houses are small but tidy. The front yards look manicured and well taken care of. In my neighborhood, Mercedes and Lexus fill the driveways. Here there are pick-up trucks and mini-vans. My neighborhood is dark at night with only the natural light of the moon and stars. In this neighborhood street lights shine down on sidewalks. Jake had looked up my address in the school directory, and after our disastrous date, I had done the same. I need to understand who Jake is, even though I'll only see his house. Maybe this is a way I can start to forget about him . . . or at least that's what I tell myself.

From the reflective numbers on the mailbox, I find his house. Every room is lit with a golden glow. A boy's bicycle is propped up against a hedge in front of the house. Three cars are wedged into the driveway, including Jake's Jeep. Parked alongside the sidewalk is a large white truck with storage containers built into its bed. *Robbins Electric: Family Owned since 1959* is sten-ciled on its side.

I feel like I'm even with Jake now. I've peeked into his life just like he peeked into mine. I wonder what he saw in me that made him ask me out. Could he ever see it again? I doubt it. Now he knows the end of the story and before he only knew the beginning. And what about me? What would I do differently if I had the chance? I just wish I had the chance. I feel sad for what

I think I've lost before I even had it. And I feel confused about what exactly *it* was.

I turn off the lights of my car several houses before I reach mine. I shut my car door as quietly as I can. I don't want anyone to know I'm home; I just want to go up to my tent and be alone. My father's probably back in bed by now and Marie will definitely be consoling him. So I'm the bad guy—a role I'm unfortunately getting used to. There are a lot of people who would agree with that—Jake being one of them, I'm sure. When I slammed Dad's bedroom door behind me it felt good, but now I feel guilty because I know how sick he must be to spend a day in bed. And I know Marie's probably mad at me for making him feel even worse.

Dr. Bronstein. I knew that name was going to come up again. How is talking to a stranger supposed to make everything better? How can it erase what's happened and my part in it? Especially when it's me doing all the talking and him doing none of the telling. Except for the part about the five stages of grief that a person has to go through . . . denial, anger, bargaining, depression, and acceptance. But even when he explained that to me I couldn't see how I fit into those neat little categories . . . although I admit I get angry a lot and I'm usually pretty depressed. The rest of it didn't make sense to me though and it sure hasn't helped.

But no sooner have I climbed the ladder to my rooftop home when the familiar marimba tune lights up my iPhone. Chad's name shows up on the screen.

"Hi Chad."

"Krista . . . I saw the Hornet in the driveway. You're back?"

"Yeah. What's up?"

"Can I come up?"

"You know you're not allowed." I almost relent but I think that would set a bad precedent. "Something wrong?"

"My mom and your dad went back to bed."

"Oh. That's good."

"I'm just watching TV."

"Mmm hmm."

"Krista. Don't be mad at Emma. She didn't mean to tell them. She's just not very good at . . . at . . ."

"At lying." I finish the sentence for him so he doesn't have to feel like he's insulting me. "I'm not mad at her—you can tell her that."

"She feels bad that she got you in trouble with Dr. Matzke."

"So weird that you call him that, Chad. Anyway . . . she didn't get me in trouble with my dad. There's just a whole lot of stuff she doesn't understand that happened before. But I don't feel like explaining it right now if that's okay with you."

"No, you don't have to explain it," he says quickly. "It's okay with me." A long pause. "Krista?"

"Yeah."

"There's something else."

"What?"

"You know how I told you that Jake guy was flirting with the girl in the store today?"

"Yes, Chad. I don't really want to talk about that either."

"Well . . . I was lying. He wasn't flirting and there wasn't any pretty girl. I don't know why I said that."

A big ache starts inside my heart and spreads through my whole chest.

"Krista?'

"Yeah?"

"Are you mad at me?"

"No, Chad. I'm not mad at you. I'll see you in the morning, okay?"

The night feels as warm, soft, and fuzzy as baby Henry's little bobblehead. The moon is so bright it's like someone took a dimmer switch to the sun and just dialed it down a bit. I lean back in my reclining chair and push my legs out in front of me. I stare up at the billions of stars and whatever it is that's beyond them. My dad says he's moving on. The policeman told me to move along. I imagine myself caught up in the ever-expanding universe. Moving away from the center—further and further. Always moving. Moving along. Moving on.

I doze off. In my dream, I'm pounding on a huge oak door with both fists, but nobody will open it.

"Leave me alone!" I cry out. "I know who you are!"

A huge owl observes me with copper-colored eyes.

"Be careful of what you don't say." The owl speaks to me. "Be careful of what you hide."

"I'm sorry!" I sob. "I'm sorry. Forgive me."

When I wake up I'm still in the lounge chair and I'm shivering. My cheeks are wet with real tears. A great-horned owl is perched on the corner of my roof, surveying the landscape below. When it hears me rustle in my chair it glides off into the night on silent wings.

I can't stop shivering although it's cool, but not cold. Even my teeth are chattering. I recognize this feeling.

For the first time since I moved to my rooftop tent, I'm afraid. I get up from my chair and crawl into the tent, zipping the entrance behind me.

Chapter | 12

When I go into the house the next morning, everyone's up and sitting around the breakfast table. A visitor would mistake this for one big happy family.

"Krista!" Marie is serving pancakes and bacon. "Sit down. Are you hungry?"

I am, and I do. My father smiles stiffly at me and then turns his attention back to the stack of pancakes in front of him.

"Sleep well?" he asks with a forced matter-of-factness in his voice.

"Yeah, I slept fine." I wonder if my father regrets what he said to me last night. Or maybe he's just giving me time for everything to sink in. This makes more sense to me. If I stay out of his way, I'll probably be able to avoid a follow-up conversation for a while. Or maybe not . . . maybe he's just getting ready to bring up Dr. Bronstein again.

Chad pours maple syrup over everything on his

plate, including the bacon. He has the soccer ball on his lap as if he's afraid someone will take it from him. It seems that all of us are conspiring to put on a show of family unity. Everyone except Emma, that is. She's pushing food around her plate with her fork but eating very little of it. She leans over and with her darting pink tongue, she creates an island of white plate in an ocean of brown syrup.

"Emma!" Marie scolds her. "Do not lick your plate. It's bad manners."

Emma looks up, mortified to be publicly called out like this. She looks at me out of the corner of her eye and I smile at her. She half-smiles nervously, probably not yet sure where she stands after her betrayal.

"Krista," she says hesitatingly, but in a way that lets me know she's ready to let me back in her life if I'm ready to do the same. "Look what I found." She scoots her chair from the table and skips into the next room returning seconds later with a lifelike porcelain-skinned doll in a long red flannel dress. A shiny auburn braid falls over one shoulder. Round blue eyes are open in perpetual wonder.

"Where did you get that?" I get up from my chair and carefully take the doll from Emma's arms.

"I . . ." She looks at her mother who looks at my father. My father says nothing, only stares straight ahead. Marie opens her mouth as if to say something but thinks better of it and then she too looks away from Emma.

"It's just that . . . It's just that you shouldn't go in people's rooms when the door is closed, that's all," I say. And then to soften it a little I add, "I'm not mad at you,

Emma, but it's not a play doll for you, okay? It's not a room for you to go in."

"Okay," she says and seems to accept.

"Do you have plans for today, Krista?" Marie is anxious to change the subject and so am I. "I'm feeling better so I thought I'd take the kids clothes shopping. Care to join us? We can stop for lunch somewhere."

"I don't want to go clothes shopping," Chad protests. "Especially not with my mom and little sister."

"Wanna go somewhere and kick the ball around, Chad?" A sudden inspiration comes to me. I don't want to stay around the house with Dad, but as usual, I have no other plans. I used to enjoy kicking the ball back in the days when I was on a soccer team.

Chad's eyes light up. "Heck yeah!"

My dad looks happy. Marie looks happy . . . and relieved. Even I feel a little happy, although my dream still feels very real to me.

I'VE DUG UP my old soccer shorts and shoes and I even find a pair of bright pink soccer socks in one of my drawers. Luckily my feet haven't grown for a while. Chad didn't come prepared for soccer so he's wearing cargo shorts and sneakers. Seeing the boy skillfully juggle the ball yesterday has clearly fired up his competitive juices.

"So where should we go?" The bad thing about living on top of a hill is the impossibility of playing any kind of ball sport. "The park?"

Chad is sitting next to me in the Hornet. He ponders this question for a moment before answering.

"Let's go to Del Oro," he says, referring to my high school. "They already have the goals set up and I can practice taking shots."

I'm not anxious to think about school during the summer, especially after that night at the pool with Jake. But it does make sense so we head off in that direction.

I'm surprised at how sharp my skills are after three years, and I'm also surprised at how good it feels to do something like this. My scalp prickles from the heat and my muscles feel warm and loose. A ribbon of moisture clings to my hairline. In another fifteen minutes, it will break loose and the sweat will drip down my forehead and temples.

"Time out!" I call to Chad. "Let's get some water."

We walk to the side of the field where a row of redwoods beckons with shade. I pull the last two water bottles from the soccer bag and toss one to Chad. We both sit down on the shaded grass and empty the contents of the bottles down our parched throats.

"Thanks for doing this, Krista. It would've sucked to go shopping."

"No problem. I'm having fun. When do you have to go home?"

"My dad's picking us up at three." Chad's world is complicated and it's his job as the older child to make it seem simple to his parents.

"So, you'll be back in two weeks? Maybe we can do this again. Bring your stuff with you next time."

"Yeah . . . and maybe you can come watch one of my games this year." I can hear the enthusiasm in his voice. In his mind, summer is over and soccer season has already begun. He looks longingly at the grassy field. "Can we go out again for a little while longer?"

I glance at my watch. It's not even noon and, although I'm getting tired, I don't want to stop either. Off in the distance I see a group of guys in maroon and yellow practice jerseys walking in our general direction. It's the football team on their way to summer practice. They'll have to pass through this field on the way to their own. They jostle each other as they walk, and laughs pass as easily between them as the footballs that are being tossed back and forth. I wonder what it would be like to be part of a group that is so united in purpose and so dependent on the goodwill its members feel toward each other.

"It's the football players!" Chad has a starry look in his eyes. "I want to play football in high school but Mom won't let me even though Dad says it's okay."

"Why won't she let you?" I nervously scan the crowd of players looking for Jake. When I spot him, I scoot further back into the shade of the redwood and press myself up against its trunk to blend in."

"She says it's too dangerous." Then, in a voice that's just a bit too loud for my comfort he blurts out, "Hey, it's Jake!"

At the sound of his name, Jake turns his head and squints into the shadow of the redwood. When his eyes adjust enough to realize who he's looking at, he lifts his hand and then lets it fall to his side. My heart pounds so furiously, I feel sure Chad must be able to hear its beat. I half-raise my hand in return.

"Maybe we should head home," I say. "I'm getting kind of hungry and you probably need to take a shower and pack up your stuff before your dad comes to get you."

Chad needs no explanation to understand that the attention he just drew to us means the end of our time here, so he doesn't complain. He also understands that it will take me a few minutes to gather up our things—the few minutes it takes for the team to continue on to their practice field.

CHAD HAS BEEN waiting out in front of our house for his father to arrive. This is the routine he's established when visiting his mother to avoid the awkwardness of bringing his parents together in the presence of their kids. I don't believe Marie ever told Chad to do this and I doubt if his father did either. He just figured it out on his own after only two visits.

When I think about Chad's routine it makes me think of the goldfish I won at my school fair when I was about Emma's age. When I brought the fish home and released it into the bowl my mother had prepared, the fish swam about, wildly testing its boundaries, familiarizing itself with the rules imposed by the shape of the glass. An hour later it was swimming calmly, having calculated exactly how far it could go in one direction before having to turn around to go in the other. It was as though the fish had never known any other home before that bowl. Chad and I have had to adapt to our new living circumstances. Emma too. I think we've all done amazingly well in such a short period of time, at least to an outside observer.

Chad comes inside to get Emma and carry their bags to the car. He gives Marie a peck on the cheek and I see a brightness in her eyes that people get when they're holding back tears. *Shiny eyes*, Mom used to call it, when I was just about to lose it over a sad book or movie. Marie leans forward and hugs Chad tightly. Then she hugs Emma and buries her face in Emma's platinum hair. Chad grabs his sister by the hand and pulls her toward the door.

"Bye, Krista," he says. "See you in a few weeks."

I haven't ever received parting words like this from Chad. As tame as the words sound, they shout out to me.

"Don't forget your soccer stuff next time," I remind him. And then before he can leave, "I'll walk you guys out to the car."

I've never done this before and I know it means something to Chad. It validates the whole other part of his life I've chosen to ignore up until now. The man waiting for them behind the wheel of the SUV wears sunglasses and is tanned and blond. He is broader and more muscular than my father who is slender, elegant, and dark. I'm not sure what I expected their dad to look like. To be honest, I've never given him a moment's thought. Now I see his broad grin and I realize he's missed his children. Their sadness about leaving their mother is forgotten as they pile into the car, pulling their bags in behind them. In two weeks' time, this same scene will replay itself.

The car pulls away and Chad rolls down his window to wave. Their father nods at me and smiles.

Chad and I have come a long way during this visit, and I'm not exactly sure why, considering what I put him through. We've been feeling our way around each other ever since Marie moved in with my dad. In the beginning, I blamed him for his mother and he blamed me for my father. But I think what clicked with both of us this time is that we have more that unites us than separates us. Because we're not adults we have to live by rules that we didn't make and we're both trying to figure out how to do that. We have to adapt before we crash into the glass bowl.

Chapter | 13

About three years ago, I had a disturbing experience. It bothered me for months and I even had nightmares about it long after that. This was before I knew what a real nightmare was and how quickly and unexpectedly it could take over a person's life. For a long time, I convinced myself that this incident was a "harbinger", a word we learned in English class that means something which is a sign for another bigger thing that's about to happen.

Does everyone have a place in their house that's a scary place? I do. My scary place is the garage, and even within the garage, there's a corner where I still won't go. But on that day I came into the garage to look for something . . . now I don't even remember what it was. Back then our garage was a mess. Boxes were scattered around the edges of where the cars pull in. There was no order to anything so if you were looking for something you just had to go poking around until you found it. On that day, it was outrageously hot, but in the garage, it was cool and dry.

I saw the box I was looking for. It was high up on one of the shelves built into the wall. I looked around for something to stand on and saw an old Lego table that Mom thought we should keep in case any little kids came to visit. I leaned over to move the Lego table and strangely heard the sound of maracas. We had a pair of maracas, along with some other percussion type instruments like miniature conga drums, and an African thumb piano. Any musical instrument we ever showed an interest in, Mom would buy for us. Too bad we had zero talent for music. But at that moment, I just wondered who was shaking the maracas, and for one crazy minute, I thought I was hearing a ghost.

And then I saw it coiled under the Lego table, maybe six inches from my hand. A huge rattlesnake, fat across its middle, head raised back, body coiled, and the tip of its tail lifted into the air, vibrating just like a pair of maracas.

This was what I dreamed of for months after . . . its eyes. Its eyes looked like pure evil to me because in them I saw nothing. And I had never seen nothing before that moment. Nothing turned out to be the scariest thing I knew.

Somehow I got my bearings. I screamed, and the snake retreated, more scared of me (they say) than I was of it. My father rushed in and killed it with a shovel. Its body continued to writhe for minutes after it was dead, and a blood stain was visible for months afterward, despite repeated attempts to bleach it out.

After that, my father completely organized the garage to eliminate any potential hiding places. He explained to me that the snake had come in to escape the heat of the day, being a cold-blooded creature. He assured me the snake was neither good nor bad. It just was. It was a living thing trying to stay alive and it had the bad fortune of being discovered by me. It wasn't a harbinger or anything else. It was simply a rattlesnake. But that part of the garage where the stain is no longer visible is a place I've avoided until today.

Now this scary place in the garage frightens me for a different reason. It's a place where secrets are stored. My family secrets. I'm here to find the journal my mother kept about my grandfather's childhood. The one with the word HOLOCAUST branded onto its cover with black marker. It seems tragic that the journal of the most innocent time in my grandfather's life should have such an ominous title.

There are some old kitchen chairs in the storage area. Mom put them here a week before the accident when we got our new kitchen set. She thought we might need them one day if we had a large party and needed extra seating, but they've never been moved from this spot. I brush away a cobweb and pull one of the chairs so it's centered under the light. With the journal in my lap, I flip open its cover and an impossibly faded photo falls from the pages. It's creased and so fragile it seems miraculous that it still exists.

I get up to turn on a second light, and the figures in the images look back at me. It's a group picture with three rows. The first row consists only of a woman sitting on the ground, holding a baby in her lap. In the second row are four boys, who look like they range from Emma's age to Chad's age. The three biggest boys are wearing caps, the kind that came back into fashion a few years ago when movie stars started wearing them— newsboy hats, they're called. In the last row three older girls are smiling over the shoulders of the younger boys in front of them. The girls could be about my age. Everyone is dressed in cold weather clothes and there's a small low building behind them.

I flip the photo over and can barely make out the scrawled old-fashioned cursive. *February 1944*, it says. *Bela (12) Miklos (8) Vili (6) Gyuri (10).* The four brothers. My grandfather, I know, is Gyuri which means George in Hungarian. And now that I know which one he is I can see the old man in the face of this little boy. The eyes are shadowed, probably from a bright winter sun directly overhead, and the focus of the picture is slightly blurred. But the way he leans timidly and yet protectively into his little brother Vili, the cocked head, the slightly crooked smile . . . how could I not recognize him? And without anything to back me up but my intuition, I suddenly know that this was the last time these young brothers stood shoulder to shoulder and smiled with all the innocence of their youth.

I thumb through the pages of the journal and find a Ziploc baggie that contains two yellowed documents. My father used to joke that if Mom came across something weak and defenseless that couldn't be cured with chicken soup and a hug, she'd put it inside a Ziploc baggie. How did he step away from all those memories to begin something new? Did he try to do it, or did it just happen to him? I never want it to happen to me . . . so do I have to accept sadness as my lifelong companion?

One of the documents is thick and rectangular. It resembles a postcard, although it looks nothing like any postcard I've ever seen. There's no tropical beach lined with coconut palms, no national park backdrop with a bear climbing through the window of a car, no Washington Monument or Lincoln Memorial. It's a strictly-business postcard and every square inch has been filled with writing as though the words were precious gems that needed to be stored somewhere—safely and quickly. The other document is just a scrap of paper, unfolded now but with so many creases it's obvious that someone sometime was trying to make it as small as possible. The writing is in pencil, large and clumsy. I can't read it but it must be Hungarian.

I don't know how many minutes have passed when I turn the last written page of the journal. After that, there are nothing but blank pages. The blank pages feel like the end of time. But they also feel like promises of more to come. Mom tried her best but she wound up with just a collection of facts. There are no personal stories. There's no emotional response to the facts. It seems to me that all this information could just as easily have been copied and pasted from an ancestry internet website. Only the clues hint at more . . . the faded picture, the postcard and the folded scrap of paper.

For as long as I can remember, Mom spoke to us about the Holocaust. She used general words designed to deliver facts without causing childhood nightmares. But Mom knew the truth even though she couldn't get past her father's vague answers and her mother's warning looks. She knew the truth of history but she didn't know the truth of the stories. And yet I can see from this notebook how hard she was trying. And I can imagine her frustration stemming from fear that time was running out—not her own, she couldn't know that, but my grandpa's. She wanted to peel back the layers and reveal those stories before it was too late. For his sake. For her sake. For our sake. Now I think I have a chance to finish what she started. Maybe it's something I can do for her.

It doesn't seem right to leave the journal in the box in this scary part of the garage. I want to read it again, but not in this place. I set the box back on the shelf and take the journal to my tent, stopping off first in the kitchen for another Ziploc baggie to protect the picture.

Chapter | 14

When I first learned in school that the sun doesn't rise and set it took me a while to grasp the concept. I saw the sun doing these very things. And I couldn't feel the earth's rotation on its axis, so I didn't believe it. The words that we use to describe the daily events—sunrise and sunset—well they just confirmed my belief.

There was something more. In my childish brain, I wanted to believe I was the center of the earth and the earth was the center of everything else. To imagine a monstrous and merciless sun commanding the planets from its stationary throne was too frightening a thought. Our earth was just a slave to the sun, and I had no more importance than a speck of dust. Even sunlight was greater than me.

But now the very thing I found frightening is a comfort. I like feeling like I'm just such a small piece of such a big puzzle. In the scale of things, my hurt is unimportant. And my happiness as well. I sit on my reclining chair and wait for the earth to rotate just a little bit more. In another hour, I'll see the bright orange ball on the western horizon, red and pink clouds coiling around it. Every leaf of every tree, every blade of grass, every bird, reptile and mammal will turn toward the sun as it disappears behind the earth's shadow. Some of its warmth will stay behind to remind us of its great power and size. The breeze on my rooftop is as soft as a whisper. How many moments will I have like this in my lifetime? How many different places will I sit to watch the sun set?

TODAY IS SUNDAY and dinner is just a sandwich I take up to my tent. Sunday dinners aren't the big deal they used to be ever since it's just been Dad and me. And now with Marie, even she doesn't mind when we all do our own thing. It's become the one night of the week when we're allowed to do that.

Tonight, I have a mission—to translate the two documents I found in the journal. Surprisingly, I've found no translation anywhere in the journal. Probably my mom understood the words and figured she'd write it down one day. She didn't know she would run out of time.

With my laptop opened to a translation site, I select *Hungarian to English*. I type the words into the Hungarian box as best as I can decipher them, not bothering with punctuation or accent marks. Like magic, as though someone was typing simultaneously, the words appear in English in the adjacent box. I have my translation of the postcard—or at least an approximation of what I can piece together that makes sense.

> *My dear family . . . I miss you all so much . . . I*
> *am here . . . able to work . . . I am fine . . . they*
> *will be moving us soon . . . please send me letters*
> *to . . . I don't know when I can . . . please don't*
> *worry about me . . . but help your mother . . . love*
> *each other my sons . . . when we are all together*
> *again . . . I love you all so much . . . a million*
> *kisses and a million more . . . love Father*

The postmark came from someplace in Hungary. My mother's journal says that my great-grandfather Jeno, was sent first to a forced-labor camp in Hungary before being sent on to Buchenwald in Germany. Technically not a death camp, Jeno nonetheless died in Buchenwald along with 33,000 others.

My mother's journal goes on to say that *Buchenwald* is the German word for "beech forest". A really pretty name if you think about it . . . especially for a place where the slogan above the entrance said "To Each His Own," but where it was understood the real meaning was "Everyone Gets What They Deserve". I wonder if Germans today talk about taking a stroll through the buchenwald—or did they invent another name for a beech forest since then?

Next I get to work translating the note written on the scrap of paper that had been folded so many times.

> *. . . heard you are here . . . I . . . happy to know*
> *you are alive and I hope well . . . if you have a*
> *shirt or any extra piece of bread . . . have eaten*

*nothing but . . . weeks . . . sick . . . take care
. . . vili . . . so young . . . careful . . . love . . . a
million kisses . . . Mother*

My mother's journal documents my great-grandmother's deportation to Auschwitz, which was a death camp. Three of her young sons were sent there as well. This note was passed from person to person, at great risk, to get from my great-grandmother Helen in one part of the camp to her eldest son Bela, who was already dead by the time it reached his barracks. After the war, it was put into the hands of my grandfather by someone who had been there. Someone from his hometown who kept it safe, knowing that one day words would be the only thing left.

I learned in school that reading between the lines is just as important as reading the lines themselves. In the postcard and the scrap of paper there is more to read between the lines than there are actual translatable words. But with just these few words, and only the context provided by Mom's journal, I feel like I've had a glimpse into a microcosm that was once a family. I feel the love and the bond and the million kisses of a mother, father, and four young sons. I learned more about Grandpa George in fifteen minutes than I learned in fifteen years. Maybe Mom wanted to share the secrets of these clues with me. But she might have thought I wasn't ready to hear them.

GRANDPA ARRIVES TOMORROW so today is my last free day with no obligations. My summer job will begin when I pick him up at the airport. This morning begins with two incoming texts. The first is from Lyla and she seems bored. I guess too much of a good thing *can* really be too much of a good thing. The second is from Chad who has achieved twenty consecutive juggles with the soccer ball.

I don't want to go back to sleep but I'm not fully awake. I'm still in that in-between state where either side could win. I visualize Chad standing on a driveway that looks exactly like Jake's driveway, except without the three cars. He has a serious, purposeful look in his eyes, and maybe the tip of his tongue is peeking out the way it does when he concentrates on something. He's counting out loud each time the top of his shoe makes contact with the ball . . . eighteen, nineteen, twenty. He stops to text me before starting over again.

And then the image of the boy at 758 seizes control of the movie that's playing inside my head. He's juggling the purple sparkly ball with his bare foot. He barely taps it in order to keep it from flying out into the street. He counts in a language I don't understand.

I sit upright and banish sleep from the tent. This is my last free day. Nobody is here to tell me what to do. I don't have any responsibilities, and I have a clear head. I know what I want to do and, no matter what Dad thinks, I know it's not wrong. I want to go back to 758. I still haven't seen him and I want to. I need to.

I DON'T NEED anyone's permission but I still feel like I should tell someone. There has to be a way for me to communicate how important this is to me. Someone should be encouraging me about this . . . obsession? But there isn't anyone, so I go to the study where Charlie squawks a greeting. I've brought a carrot tip and a slice of apple which I place on his fresh produce dish. He clambers down from his perch to the floor of the cage, using his beak the way an old man would use a cane. He begins to munch, at the same time keeping an eye on me.

"Charlie, just so you know, I'm going back there."

I must be crazy talking to a bird.

"Everyone wants me to move on, but you under-stand, don't you, guy? You can't move on either."

And then, as if to illustrate the point, I stick my finger in the cage and Charlie scurries away to the farthest corner.

I DRIVE DOWN the street prepared to make my usual U-turn to park in my usual place on the opposite side of the street facing the wrong way. The faded brown Toyota is in the driveway again. I'm sure that means he's home, so I've gotten lucky today. If he leaves, I'll see him. When it happens, I'll know what to do. In the meantime, I just have to stay calm.

But before I engage the parking brake, I hear a whoop and a red light flashes behind me. When the door of the police car opens, I can see it's the same cop who spoke to me last week. In my side mirror, I watch him as he approaches. He motions for me to roll down the window.

"Are we going to go through this again?" he asks. He looks tired.

"You said I wasn't breaking the law. And this is a public street." I refuse to be forced away this time. I'm also wondering if the commotion I'm causing will bring *him* out of his house.

"You know they could get a restraining order against you." He pushes his sunglasses on top of his head and I can see his eyes—vivid blue and kind. "You don't want that to happen, do you?"

"*They* can get a restraining order against *me*. That's funny."

"You didn't answer my question." The sun causes him to squint so he pulls his sunglasses back over his eyes. "Do you want these people to get a restraining order against you, because that's what I'm going to advise them to do."

"No." I look straight ahead.

"No what?"

"No, sir."

He laughs quietly. "I didn't mean that. I meant: no, you don't want them to get a restraining order against you: or no, you're not going to leave?"

I think about it for a few seconds with my eyes on 758. I have to stay strong.

"Both," I say finally.

"Stay here, I'll be right back." He walks over to his car and gets inside.

I can see in my rearview mirror that he's talking to someone on his radio. After a few minutes he comes back. There's been no sign of activity at 758. No shadows behind the window or children playing in the yard.

He leans over to talk through my window. "Lock up

your car and come with me."

"Am I under arrest?" The injustice is hard to believe.

"No, you're not under arrest. This is your lucky day 'cause you get to come on a ride-along with me. I just had to clear it with my platoon commander."

I make no move to get out of my car. This isn't exactly what I would consider my lucky day and a ride-along is the last thing I want to do right now.

"I'm a little nervous about leaving my car here." Still nothing happening across the street.

His mouth pulls to one side into a who-are-you-kidding expression.

"Let's go," he says. "Before I decide to stop being so nice."

I take my time getting out of the Hornet and locking up. If the brown Toyota wasn't parked in the driveway, I'd think nobody was home. The man who lives next door has come out of his house. He makes a production of going to his mailbox and standing beside it while he opens and reads each letter, but he's really just watching us. I follow the policeman to his patrol car and get in through the passenger side door.

"Where are we going? I'm not in the mood for a high-speed chase or a shoot-out."

"By the way my name is Officer Jensen and you can call me Officer Jensen."

I guess he thinks he's funny. "I'm Krista Matzke."

"I know who you are. Remember, I saw your driver's license last week."

He flips the blinker signal and turns right onto El Dorado, a busy six-lane street that's lined on both sides with bowling alleys, fast-food restaurants, warehouse stores and dingy stucco apartment buildings that might have been pink at one time but now look kind of gray.

"Do you know I went to the same high school as you?" he asks.

"You went to Del Oro?" For some reason, this surprises me. I guess he just looks out of context in his uniform in this place. "That must have been a long time ago."

He smiles and shakes his head. "I graduated ten years ago. My ten-year reunion is next month."

We've stopped at a red light. Outside my window is a do-it-yourself car wash—the kind where you feed quarters into a coin box and you spritz soapy water on your car until your time runs out, so you have to move fast. My father took me to one of those when I was younger. He let me hold the wand and spray the car, only he forgot to close the window all the way. I thought I would get in trouble, but he just laughed about it and we dried the inside with a blanket we got from the trunk of the car.

Now I take my car to a car wash where they serve Italian sodas, espressos, and biscotti. They play movies on flat screen monitors and keep all the current celebrity magazines and newspapers in the waiting room. When your car is ready, they announce it on the loudspeaker. But it was fun that time Dad took me to the do-it-yourself car wash.

"How do you know where I go to high school? Does it say that in your computer?"

"Krista, I know who you are and I know what you're doing." He pauses and takes a deep breath. "I was working that day. We all heard about what happened. A friend of mine from police academy was one of the first responders."

"What am I doing?"

"What?" We've turned into a rundown strip mall and he drives slowly through the parking lot. Four or five boys about my age are gathered near the front of a liquor store. When they see the patrol car approaching they stare blankly until we pass. One of them catches my eye and smiles right at me. He's handsome and has shiny black hair that's combed straight off his face. He kisses his fingertips and blows across them in my direction.

"You said you know what I'm doing. I'm just asking you to explain."

"Let me clarify. I'm not a hundred percent sure what your motives are, but if I had to guess I'd say you're trying to make life just a little bit uncomfortable for Omar Aziz."

"And is that a bad thing?"

"It's borderline breaking the law. And depending on how far you plan on going, the answer is yes, that could be a bad thing." He pulls out of the parking lot back onto busy El Dorado. "So how far were you planning on going?"

"I just wanted to see him. I didn't plan anything beyond that." I don't want to use his name even though Officer Jensen has introduced it into the car—kind of like letting a bobcat out of a trap, it feels like it's loose now, and dangerous.

"Krista, I'm going to tell you some things about Omar that you might already know. Just hear me out, okay?"

I don't want to know anything about him. I know enough.

"I'm taking your silence as an 'okay.'" Officer Jensen is very by-the-book, and yet, not by-the-book. I try to envision him walking through the hallways of Del Oro, stopping at the water fountain for a quick drink before the bell rings. I imagine him in the boys' locker room where Jake took me that night. Officer Jensen was one of the ghosts whose presence I felt, joking around with his friends in the physical way boys have of communicating with each other.

"Do I have a choice?"

"Yes, you do. So stop me anytime." As we drive, all the cars around us slow down to match our pace. "Omar was just shy of eighteen at the time of the accident, but he'd only had his driver's license for six months."

"I know."

"He was working three jobs at the time, Krista. *Three* jobs. And he had dropped out of school six months earlier so he could hold down those three jobs."

"Boo-hoo."

"His family was granted political asylum to come here from Afghanistan because his father had been a translator for U.S. troops. He was murdered by the Taliban, leaving behind a pregnant wife and two kids. Sort of a message to the people of that village not to cooperate with the Americans—Omar saw his father hanging in the village square."

I sigh loudly. I pretty much know all about this. "When he got his driver's license, he didn't learn that it's illegal to text while you're driving?"

"He was delivering a pizza, and his boss texted him

to find out what was taking him so long. He knew he was breaking the law but his mind was on his job—so he made the very bad decision to text him back." We were driving down smaller streets now, heading back toward 758.

"The very bad decision," I repeat. "How about the decision that pretty much destroyed the rest of my life?"

"You're young, Krista. Trust me when I tell you that you're going to have a life. You'll never get back what you lost but you can go on with what you have now—and build on it."

"Two years. Two years is enough to pay for what he did?"

"That was the judge's decision. To try him as a minor. To take into account his history and circumstances."

"Circumstances?"

"That his family is dependent on him for financial support. That he's helping his mother raise his younger brother and sister."

We pull up behind the Hornet and Officer Jensen leaves his engine running.

"I'm going to watch you until you get into your car and drive away," he says. "And I don't want to see you back here, okay? If I do, I *will* advise the Aziz family that they have the right to file for a restraining order against you. And if they do, and you violate the restraining order, you *will* be arrested."

"It's not fair." My eyes are burning with unshed tears.

"Nothing in life is fair. I see evidence of that every day."

I step out of the patrol car and start to close the door.

"Krista." Officer Jensen lifts his sunglasses and looks straight into my eyes. "Don't ever believe his punishment ends after two years. He'll punish himself for the rest of his life."

As I pull away from the curb I look one last time at 758. The brown Toyota is gone.

The House on Fire

Chapter | 15

When I get home, I suspect I'm in a shit-load of trouble. My dad's car is in the driveway and it's not even three o'clock. I have a feeling he's heard from Officer Jensen and I'm tempted to sneak up to my tent, but I know that's putting off the inevitable, so I go inside.

When I see Dad, I really do feel sorry for him, which surprises me because that's never happened before. No matter what I've felt about him in the past, he's always seemed strong to me. Now he looks frail, kind of beat down. He almost looks . . . old.

"Krista." He's sitting at the kitchen table with a cup of coffee he's made for himself. "What are we going to do about you?"

"About . . . *me*?" I stand until he motions for me to sit down. We face each other across the table.

"I asked you to stay away from that house." Apparently, my father can't bring himself to use the name either. "I've asked you to go back to counseling. What am I supposed to do with you?"

"I don't know. I guess I'm kind of inconvenient, aren't I?"

"Stop it! You know I love you. Marie loves you too. She tries so hard with you."

"Tries what? To love me? She doesn't love me—she only wants to get you to marry her."

"That's enough!" His voice rises and then softens immediately. "I'm trying, I really am . . . but I can't be both father *and* mother to you. You need a mother, honey, and Marie wants to be your mother if you'll just give her a chance."

"Why doesn't she try being a mother to Emma and Chad for a start?" My father slams his coffee cup on the table and glares at me. At the sound of that cup crashing down, something inside me snaps and I feel anger rising from deep inside, almost like a volcano that's about to erupt. My cheeks are hot and there's a roaring sound in my ears. I can't stop what I know is going to happen next—I'm losing it. "I don't need *a* mother!" My voice is so loud now the neighbors can probably hear. "I need *my* mother!" The words tear at my throat like pieces of shrapnel.

"Well you *can't* have her!" The volume of my father's voice now matches my own, in fact, it exceeds it. His face turns almost purple, and veins pop out on both temples. "Your mother is *dead*, Krista. She's *dead*! You think you're the only one who suffered, Krista? I lost half my family too!"

The terrible words have been spoken. My father and I have always been careful to use our safe words like 'gone' or 'lost to us' or 'not with us anymore.' But now that he's broken our unspoken agreement, I suddenly feel I can't breathe. My father buries his head in his hands and sobs.

I run from the kitchen only wanting to get away from him and that terrible word that came out of his mouth. When I pass by his bedroom, a horrible thought comes to me and I walk into his bathroom. I know where the sleeping pills are, and I shuffle through the various medicines until I find them. Then I empty the entire contents of the bottle into the palm of my hand and stare at them—imagining them in my mouth, imagining gulping down the water that would force them down my throat, into my stomach, through my veins, to my heart, to my brain. Peace at last. Peace . . . at . . . last. I fling them into the sink and turn the tap water on full blast. I throw the empty medicine bottle on the marble floor with such ferocity, the plastic splinters into shards.

"Aahhh!" I scream. "I hate . . . I hate . . ." I'm so scared and so confused. My breathing comes fast and shallow. The room is spinning. My arms and legs are numb and tingling. My mouth is bone dry and my heart is racing so fast it seems impossible it won't burst.

And then I feel my father's arms encircle me from behind. He hugs me tightly against his body.

"It's okay, honey," he says. "Just breathe. Breathe slowly. It's okay." He strokes my hair and I begin to relax. I turn around and fall into his arms, sobbing against his chest. He's crying too and we stand like that—crying in each other's arms.

"We've lost so much, Krista . . . so much. I thought I could be strong enough for both of us . . . pull us both through. I'm so sorry I've let you down."

It makes me feel sad that Dad thinks he can unfeel my feelings for me. But it doesn't surprise me.

Afterward, he leads me to the divan in his bedroom. We lean back and he just holds me tight and says nothing. My breathing is so ragged that an involuntary sob comes every few breaths. I think I actually fall asleep for a few minutes. When I open my eyes, Dad looks down at me.

"Let's go see if Rachel is home," he says quietly. "I'd like to meet the baby."

When I was a freshman in high school and on the cusp of popularity, I was chosen to be a guide for a visiting Australian student. A group of twenty high school students from Australia was attending our school for a week and each one was assigned a guide to shadow from class to class. This was an opportunity for them to see what life was like for their American counterparts. I was flattered to be chosen because the teachers recommended student guides based on their grades and citizenship—a fancy way of saying you never caused any problems in class. But maybe they also saw something in me that I didn't see in myself.

The student assigned to me was a fifteen-year-old girl named Annie. She was fun, down-to-earth, pretty in a natural way—we could have been friends. She was so interested in everything she saw. Gym class, lunch in the cafeteria, math, English . . . it all seemed to fascinate her. And the two of us attracted a lot of attention from the other students that week.

The first three days I was on a high and Lyla kidded me about how talkative I was because I normally tend to be on the quiet side. Annie came to watch my swim practice and she worked out with us on that first day. By Thursday, I was withdrawing a little—I could even see it in myself. Annie asked me why I was so quiet that day. She just assumed the Krista she saw the first three days was the normal Krista and, I must admit, I enjoyed playing that role.

I tried to analyze it later, after Annie was gone, back to the continent where water supposedly goes down the drain in the opposite direction and animals hop and carry babies in their pouches. At first, I thought it was because I knew her visit was coming to an end and I'd never see her again, so why bother putting effort into a friendship that could never go anywhere. And there may have been a little of that.

A few months ago, I thought about it again. I realized that when Annie came, I saw everything through her eyes. My world that was so familiar to me—the kids I grew up with, the way we talk and dress, the food we like, the TV shows we watch—all of those were new and exciting to Annie. I got to see my life through her eyes and it was like being on the outside looking in. All the things I took for granted became new and interesting again. But after a few days, as Annie got used to my life, I went back to being used to it as well. And, even though I loved my life, that feeling . . . that rush was gone.

Sitting here in the living room of the Sullivans' house, watching my father and Rachel drift back toward each other after a year of separation, I have a smile on my face, if not quite fully in my heart. It amazes me to realize how comfortably my opposing emotions co-exist inside of me, so that fear can easily make way for courage when the time is right—and hatred will do the same for love.

I'm holding baby Henry against my shoulder and patting him lightly on his tiny back. Picking him up was easy this time—I wanted to do it. I pull my head back to look into his wise, steely-blue eyes, and I remember again what it feels like when every day is new and life isn't taken for granted.

Chapter | 16

Today I'll pick up my grandpa from the airport, but right now it's just my dad and I sitting down together for breakfast. We don't talk about what happened yesterday, but I think we both feel like some of the pressure that was building has been released. I know my father was disappointed whe n I went up to my tent after dinner last night. I'm sure he hoped we'd made enough progress to bring me back into the house. But to his credit, he doesn't say anything about it and I know he's trying hard to understand me.

My father gives me a piece of paper that lists the doctor's appointments he's scheduled for my grandfather, beginning with a visit to his own office tomorrow. After breakfast, he excuses himself and clears his dishes. I wash the morning dishes and tidy up the kitchen. Then I go to the guest room and put clean sheets on the bed that Chad uses when he's here, and I set out clean towels and a few water bottles in the guest bathroom. Emma and Chad will have to sleep in my room while my grandpa is here. They only come every other weekend so one of them can use the air mattress. While I'm working, my father comes in to say goodbye. He gives me a big hug and a kiss on top of my head. Yesterday was traumatic for both of us, so much so that it almost feels like a physical injury. We're both being careful with each other, as though our bruises are visible.

My grandpa's plane arrives at three-thirty so I have an empty morning. Empty mornings haven't been great for me lately but this one will be different. My new goal is not really to make good things happen. It's just to make bad things not happen. It doesn't seem like a big deal but it is. I have a plan to achieve this goal that was partly inspired by Chad. The morning we spent kicking the soccer ball felt great—that is, until the football team arrived. Running, sweating, focusing on the physical side of me changed me for a few hours and I remember that sensation. Maybe it's true that endorphins released during exercise provide a temporary feeling of well-being. I plan to test that theory this morning.

It's still early enough the day isn't too hot. I step out into the street wearing my running shoes, shorts, and t-shirt. My hair is pulled away from my face and neck into a pony-tail high on my head. Rachel is at the end of her driveway, bent over picking up her newspaper from the ground. She sees me when she straightens up and I make a small circular wave with my open hand. She points to her chest, makes a heart sign with both index fingers and thumbs and then points to me. For some reason, sign language feels better than spoken words today.

I take off jogging down the street, planning to

only run our neighborhood loop today. But when the two-mile loop is done, I still feel toxic energy that needs to be burned away, so I jog down the steep hill that leads toward town. After about twenty minutes, I'm on the main street and I'm feeling muscles come to life that haven't been called on to perform for a long time. The sun is almost overhead, sweat is dripping into my eyebrows, and my back is drenched. I feel warm and loose—like nothing can stop me—but I haven't brought any water and I still have that hill to climb on the way back. I pick out a tree as my turn-around point and just as I round it, a Jeep drives by the same color as Jake's. It goes by so fast I don't have time to be sure it's his. There must be a lot of Jeeps the same color as Jake's in this town but I never had a reason to notice them before.

The hill on the way back is intense, and I have to walk some of it. A well-meaning neighbor slows down and offers me a ride but I shake my head and smile in between gasps of breath. By the time I get to my house I'm so exhausted, it's an effort to walk. I think my plan has worked. All those things tumbling around in my head are still tumbling around. I'm not exactly happy, but I'm not sad either.

Traffic on the bridge was worse than I expected for early afternoon and I was already running a little late to begin with—not exactly a promising start to the first day of my "job." When I pull up to the Passenger Arrival area at the airport, Grandpa's already cleared customs and is waiting at the curb. We're in fog country now so, although there's nothing but sunshine where I live, here in San Francisco it's cold, gray, and windy.

It's been several years, but Grandpa looks the same

to me. He's on the short side and I'm pretty sure I'm at least two or three inches taller than him now. He's bald, but has grown the right side of his hair long enough to comb over to the left side in order to cover the bald spot. But with the wind blowing the way it is, that plan has backfired and I see him put a hand up to his head to force the hair back into place. He seems a little less round than I remember him, but that's still his general shape.

When I catch my first glimpse of him, it reminds me of something I've lost, and I realize that he and I are starting all over with each other now—almost like we're meeting for the first time. He's seriously underdressed in a Hawaiian short-sleeved shirt and dark blue slacks. His head is down and he's sort of marching in place like he's trying to keep himself warm. I feel guilty for being late. Everyone should feel welcomed when they arrive in a new place. Someone should be waiting for them with open arms, a meaningless greeting like "how was your flight?", and maybe even some kind of present—or at least an offer to carry your bag. I haven't done any of these things for Grandpa.

I tap on the horn as I pull to the curb and Grandpa looks up surprised. I hop out of the car and walk around to greet him, and I'm suddenly feeling very shy of this man who's only a few degrees away from being a complete stranger. Neither of us is comfortable enough to embrace but we take a clumsy stab at it.

"Hi, Grandpa." I feel like a giantess standing next to him.

He looks me up and down. "You've grown up." His strong Hungarian accent is just as I remember it.

"Let me take your bag."

But his masculine pride won't allow it, and he grapples with his bag, struggling to lift it into the Hornet's cramped back seat.

"So you will be my driver?" he says once we're strapped in and on our way.

I'm a little embarrassed by that question but I just smile and nod my head.

"At your service." I'm trying to be flippant and funny, but I don't do either of those very well.

"It's summer here, or winter?" His eyebrows raise at the sight of the thick fog that surrounds us.

"Don't worry, it's hot where we live. San Francisco is always like this in the summer."

"Yes, I remember this."

It's a long drive back to my house and I scramble for what to say next. "Dad told me . . ." I start to say just as he starts talking. "I'm sorry. What were you going to say?"

"No, no, you," he waves me on.

"Oh. I was just going to say that Dad told me you aren't feeling well. What's wrong?"

"I'm very tired all the time," he says in a voice that's very tired. "And my friends tell me that I look peel."

I try to puzzle this one out. I don't want to offend him by not understanding.

"Your friends tell you that you're looking . . ."

"Peel!" he says with emphasis as though he's just proved a point. When I realize he means *pale*, I take a quick sideways glance to see if it's true—and it is.

"Oh." I'm not sure how to respond. "Well, Dad is a good doctor and he'll be able to find out if anything's wrong, but hopefully it's nothing." I sound stupid even to myself. My grandfather wouldn't fly to another continent if his symptoms were just nothing.

"I've gotten too used to good weather," he says.

"Is that why you and Grandma moved back to Venezuela—the nice weather?"

"That and also some other things. It's where your grandmother and I met each other and started our life together, you understand? There were many good memories. Cheap to live and beautiful country. This country took me in when I had nowhere else to go."

I look at him from the corner of my eye. He stares out the window as we're crossing the bridge high above the San Francisco Bay. The water is dark gray and choppy, but we've left the thickest of the fog behind and there are scattered patches of blue sky in front of us.

Unless I'm with Lyla or someone else I'm totally comfortable with, I'm not the greatest conversationalist. So, at some point, I learned that asking questions is a way to fill the silent gaps and people usually appreciate the attention. With Grandpa though, I'm not sure how much he'll like it. I remember my grandmother stepping in to wave off Mom when the interview went too long. So I begin with mundane things.

"Why did you leave Venezuela in the first place?"

"We applied for visas to the United States. Everyone wanted to go there. We thought it would be a good thing for your mother to be an American."

I kind of already knew this but it fills in a few blanks. He looks over at me—a little suspiciously, or is that my imagination?

"I think you must be hungry," he projects onto me.

"Let's stop before we get home and I buy you some dinner."

I don't think Dad and Marie will mind if I text and let them know. They were just going to pick something up on the way home anyway.

"What kind of food do you like?" I ask.

"Do you have Chinese restaurant? I like Chinese food—you?"

"Me too." Well, at least we have one thing in common beyond our DNA.

Grandpa's a lot more comfortable now that we're beyond the hills that trap the fog, turning the bay into a giant bowl full of mist. At last he's wearing the right clothes for the right weather. He even wants to sit outside in the back patio of the restaurant. A little creek runs behind us. It's almost dry this time of year, but in the winter, it swells and muddy brown water tears through its banks.

There's a banquet of plates set before us—Grandpa has seriously over-ordered but we can take it home and have it for lunch tomorrow.

"You're too tinny," he announces after studying me carefully. "Eat some more . . . please."

It hasn't taken long for me to pick up on the accent I remember from my childhood, so I know that tinny is thin. I also recall stories my mother told of my grandfather's obsession with food and making sure everyone got enough of it . . . something left over from *his* childhood. My father is so different. He's lean and athletic and encourages me to eat light and healthy and to push away from the table as soon as I'm satisfied. But he's never had to go without food like my grandpa.

"I don't think I can, Grandpa. My stomach's not big enough."

"No, it's not," he states sadly. "That's no good for a girl. You want to find a husband one day, no?"

I let that one pass with an awkward smile. Agree to disagree and all.

"Your father tells me you have some problems," he says out of the blue, catching me completely off-guard.

"Like what kind of problems did he tell you I'm having?" I had counted on Dad's phone conversations with Grandpa to revolve around health issues. I thought I'd have an opportunity to reinvent myself for someone who hadn't been around and seen me these last few years.

"He says you've been going to the Afghan boy's house—this Omar." Apparently, my grandfather has no difficulty in speaking his name out loud. "He's out of prison, no?"

"No. I mean yes. Yes, he's out of prison and yes I've gone by his house a few times."

"Why you go there?"

How do I answer? Because I can't pry him out of my mind? Because I think about him every day running around free—doing whatever he wants? Because I want to make him suffer, and if my presence outside his house makes him suffer even a fraction of what he's made me suffer then it will be worth it? Because I need to see him, I need to put a real face to the name—a face that I can pin all my hate on.

But how can I say all that and still come across as a rational human being?

I shrug my shoulders. "Just curious, I guess."

My grandfather chews slowly and swallows. Then he sips his iced tea. The red plastic cup is sweating from condensation and a few drops of water fall onto his shirt. He puts the cup down on the table and looks directly into my eyes.

"Let's go there right now—you and me." He waves at the waitress and motions for a check. "Are you ready?"

"No, Grandpa, we can't do that. I'll be arrested if I go there again. You probably would be too if you were with me."

"You think I'm afraid to be arrested?" He speaks slowly and raises his eyebrows as if he's unable to believe I would think something as simple as threat of arrest could stop him. "You think your grandfather is afraid of a policeman in America? You should come see what the police do in Venezuela!"

I suppress a laugh, trying hard not to think about my plump little grandpa fighting off the cops.

"It's not a good idea," I say as seriously as I can.

"So then it's your decision. We just forget about that place and that young man."

"It's my decision not to go there. But I can't forget about him." I don't want my grandfather to think that I've caved. I just want him to know I'm being practical.

"No, you can't forget." Grandpa pulls some caramels out of his pocket and offers me one. When I shake my head 'no', he proceeds to unwrap the clear cellophane from the candy. It's a complicated procedure and takes him a while. He's totally focused on it.

"Never forget," he says in a way that makes it seem like he's talking to himself. The wrapper is fully removed and he pops the caramel in his mouth. He chews with a thoughtful look in his eye. "You're a good cook?"

"No, I don't know how to cook." I'm a little embarrassed by this admission. "Maybe some scrambled eggs or French toast . . ."

"You have never made a soup?"

"No, not really."

"Pity your mother never taught you to cook. She was a good cook."

"Yeah. She was."

"If you take a small cup of water and add a few spoons of salt, you wouldn't drink this. It would be too much salt."

"Yeah, I guess so."

"But if you add juices from carrots and tomatoes and some other vegetables, then you stir in the broth of the chicken, and maybe some cream, and some more water." He has a faraway look in his eyes as though he's in the kitchen adding the ingredients as he speaks. "And then you taste it and now it tastes good. You can drink a whole bowl of it."

I'm watching my grandpa carefully because I know this is not about soup.

"So don't forget—never forget. But you add. Keep adding to your life—a little bit this, a little bit that. The salt is still there, but one day you won't notice."

Chapter | 17

Armed with enough leftovers to feed my father and Marie, we walk down the street toward the meter where the Hornet is parked. It's a gentle day, quickly giving way to a dreamy night and the sidewalks are crowded with moviegoers and early diners. It's always like this in the summer, no matter what day of the week. I feel like walking some more but I can tell my grandpa is tired and I don't want to push him. He's come a long way today and would probably like to climb into a comfortable bed.

Walking in the same direction across the street is a group of about ten kids and I recognize a few of them. The shiny-haired girls with the perfect lip gloss color to match their perfectly manicured nails. There are guys with them too—the usual ones they hang out with. They're not in my world and I'm not in theirs either, but our orbits sometimes intersect in school, just like a Venn diagram.

Today, I have to look at them. An aura surrounds them like a glistening, protective bubble. They glide down the sidewalk impervious to loneliness, shyness, and misfortune. Their smiles are shields and their laughter is a barrier against imposters. I envy their ability to free themselves within the group. Their effortlessness at belonging.

A girl breaks away from her friends and takes the arm of a boy in a black and orange baseball cap. She lowers her head and one shoulder in a submissive posture of flirtation as she looks up at him and beams. She's inviting his attention but he keeps his shoulders squared and strong. He tilts his ear politely toward her words and then, smiling, returns his attention to the friend at his side. Sensing her pull on him wasn't strong enough, she surrenders her position by his side and melts back into the inner circle of girls.

My grandfather and I have arrived at the Hornet, and I remotely unlock the door. Across the street the group of kids waits for the light to turn green and the boy in the black and orange cap looks over at my car. Then he looks at me and I can see it's Jake. The only sign of recognition he makes is the instant he holds my gaze. Then he looks away and my grandpa and I climb into the car and drive away.

Dad and Marie are waiting by the time we get home. Polite introductions are made because my grandfather has never known Marie as my father's lover. Perhaps he met her in the past as my father's nurse but I don't want to ask. This must be awkwardly painful for him.

I take him to the guest room and ask if he needs anything. I point out the phone by his bed and show him how to use the remote control for the TV. I remind him that his appointment with my father is at eleven the following morning. We purposely scheduled it a little late so he can sleep in if he needs to adjust to the time change.

Just as I'm about to leave, my grandfather remembers the bird.

"Charlie," he says. "Can I see him please?" He remembers how much my mother loved her bird.

But when he gets a look at Charlie, a mask of concern comes over his face. I explain how we're working on returning him to good health but my grandfather's first instinct is to ask if he's being properly fed. I assure him Charlie gets a variety of fruits, vegetables, vitamins, and seed.

"It's a mental thing," I explain. I stick my finger into the cage but Charlie looks away scornfully. "My goal is to get him on my finger."

"We will do this together." My grandpa has certainty in his voice. "Let me think about it tonight. Now, please show me *your* room."

I'm embarrassed. It was inevitable that he'd find out where I sleep, but it's difficult to tell this eighty-two-year-old man from Venezuela that I've pitched a tent on the roof of the garage. But since I have to tell him, I do.

"What?" His expression is horrified. "You could walk while you're sleeping and fall and be killed! Your father allows this?"

"It's okay, Grandpa. I don't sleepwalk. I'm fine. I like it up there."

I think he gets it right away though, because he doesn't ask any more questions.

"How do I talk to you if I need to?"

"This is my cell phone number." I jot it down on

a slip of paper. "Call me anytime, and I'll be down in thirty seconds."

"Pity I can't visit you. But I'm too old to climb to the roof."

Still he wants to walk outside with me and see how I get up there. He examines the ladder carefully and gives it a good shake to make sure it's sturdy.

"My father had a contractor secure both ends of the ladder. It won't slip."

"Tanks God for that." He lingers like there's something more he wants to say. "I *see* you in the morning, Kicsi."

His arms raise up slightly as if to embrace me, but only one arm comes all the way up, and he uses it to pat me on the back. I think I detect a sheen of moisture on the surface of his eyes, but maybe it's just the reflection of the moon. I breathe deeply to melt away the lump in my throat. *Kicsi* was the special nickname my grandfather used to call Mom.

MY PHONE IS ringing and it's only eight o'clock. It's Grandpa and he's wondering when I'll be down. He's worried that three hours isn't long enough for me to get ready and get him to my dad's office on time. I imagine he's nervous. He also wants to tell me about his morning so far.

"I have eaten a good breakfast prepared for me by Marie," he begins. "And I have shaved and taken my shower and washed the breakfast dishes. After your father and Marie left, the doorbell rang and a beautiful lady with her baby bring a plate of cookies for me!" I can hear the smile in his voice over the phone. "I will share with you if you come right now."

Then he adds slyly, "I have surprise for you, but you should come quickly to see it before you get ready."

When we finish talking, a text comes in from Chad:

> Can I stop by for a few minutes tonight? I have
> something to show you.

Everyone with the surprises today.

When I walk into the house, Grandpa is waiting anxiously. He hands me one of Rachel's home-baked cookies and takes me by the hand, leading me to his room. The door of his bedroom is closed and he opens it very slowly and cautiously. He has moved Charlie's cage from the study to the top of the desk in his room. The cage door is wide open and Charlie is standing on top of the dresser pecking away at one of Rachel's cookies. There's a terrible mess of crumbs all around him, but neither Charlie nor my grandfather seem to be concerned.

"He spent the whole morning out here with me," Grandpa beams with pride. "I just read my book and Charlie come out and walk around the room."

"That's fantastic, Grandpa. He looks really . . . happy."

I extend my finger in front of Charlie, but he's busy with the cookie and he moves away from me a little to continue his cookie crumb grazing.

"It takes some time. We start this way." Grandpa, the bird whisperer. "Now you need to go get ready."

"I'm going to take a quick run first. I won't be too long. Maybe thirty minutes to an hour."

"We will be late!" He looks stricken.

"No, we'll be fine. It takes me fifteen minutes to shower and dress. And Dad's office is only a ten-minute drive away."

"But you must eat!"

"I just ate that cookie and I'll grab a banana or some fruit after I run."

"This is no good. No wonder you're so tinny." Then he perks up. "Okay, you go run and Charlie and I will read together until you get back."

I'm sore from my last run but after about ten minutes I don't feel it anymore. Why haven't I done this before? I can't completely explain the feeling but I suppose it's something like this—I'm making myself stronger to prepare for . . . life? The loop around my neighborhood goes by in a flash and then I'm down the hill and already to the turn-around tree before I know it. This time I jog nearly all the way up the hill before I have to stop to walk. When I get to the top, I still have enough energy to do a half-loop cool-down. I'm sweating profusely by the time I pass the Sullivans' house.

Rachel's standing in her front yard watering some plants with the garden hose. Henry is on her back in a carrier with a little sun shade canopy. When I run by, she points the nozzle of the hose up into the air and water arcs over the sidewalk, reflecting the spectrum of light and forming a rainbow bridge. A hummingbird darts through its mist and disappears into a blossoming bush. I run under the arch of cool spray before Rachel turns the hose back to her garden.

"Did you have a cookie?" she calls after me.

"Yes. Yummy. Thanks, Rachel!" It feels so good to have her back in my life.

Chapter | 18

I don't think I've ever sat in my father's waiting room as a patient before. It's a surreal experience. I ring the bell at the counter and the window slides open to reveal Marie.

"Oh, hi Krista. Glad you guys are here early. Could you give these forms to your grandfather and ask him to fill them out please?"

I take the forms back to my grandfather knowing that I'll probably be filling them out for him. A few other patients are waiting—an older man and his wife, probably around my grandfather's age, and a young woman who's lost in a celebrity gossip magazine.

"We're actually running a few minutes behind, so don't rush." Marie slides the frosted glass window shut, leaving the five of us to politely ignore each other in the waiting room.

"You write for me, please," my grandfather says when he sees the forms. "My handwriting is not so good."

I fill in the basic information that I know and then begin to whisper the remaining questions to him. But my grandpa can't hear the whispering and asks me to speak louder. I'm a little embarrassed by the proximity of strangers in the waiting room, and, directing a look at the young woman beside us, I ask him if he wants to go out in the hallway. He looks confused for a minute as he follows my gaze to the woman, but once he gets my meaning, he speaks out loud, without lowering the volume of his voice.

"No. We stay here. I don't want to miss if Marie calls for me and I'm not here. This nice young lady cares nothing about my business."

A warm flush springs to my cheeks as a smile creeps across the woman's face.

We go through the height and weight—neither of which I can translate from metric, so I just leave them blank. Then we get to the health history and I read out a series of afflictions, all of which he answers "No" to. The door to the inner office opens and a man in a business suit exits. My father's nurse, Stella, follows him out and calls the older couple by name. The woman stands with difficulty—her husband holds her arm as she shuffles through the doorway.

"How are you today?" Stella greets them brightly. "Do you need a wheelchair?"

My grandfather and I go back to the forms.

"What symptoms bring you here today?" I read.

"I tell you . . . I am peel and very tired." My grandfather seems to talk to the form itself, and is annoyed by its silly questions. Shouldn't it know what brings him here today?

"Is there anything else you want to add that we haven't asked about today?"

He pauses to consider this and then answers in a firm voice that seems to reverberate around the room and boomerangs back to us.

"Hemorrhoids," he says almost proudly. "I get the hemorrhoids sometime when I strain for my bowel movement."

The woman beside us is still staring at the gossip magazine. She unsuccessfully tries to suppress another smile, but the result is that her lips twist into a demonic sneer. I feel a ridiculous urge to take a stand of some sort on my grandfather's behalf.

"Do you know how to spell this word?" He seems concerned that my inability to spell it will throw off his entire diagnosis.

Stella appears in the doorway and summons the young woman with the gossip magazine.

"That's okay, Grandpa, I'm pretty sure I have it right." Even though I seriously have no idea.

IT'S A LONG time before Grandpa emerges from my father's inner office. I never have to wait to see the doctor and now I know what other people go through. I'm also much more nervous than I thought I'd be about what the news will be. Grandpa emerges with a fistful of lab slips and Marie slides the window open to talk to us.

"Krista, can you get him over to the lab right now and take care of these tests? I've made a rush notation so hopefully we can get some of the results back before closing today."

Marie hands me a slip of paper with a to-do list from my father. It includes a stop at the post office to drop off some packages and a shopping list for the grocery store. There are other less important tasks which I can probably put off until tomorrow.

By the time we're done with the lab tests, my grandfather is exhausted and wants to go home. He goes straight to his room, and when I knock lightly on his door a few minutes later, there's no answer. I crack the door open and peek inside—Grandpa's sound asleep and Charlie is standing on the bed cover by his feet. This will be a good time to run to the grocery store and post office, so I jot down a note for him and leave it by his bedside table. My phone vibrates in my purse and I close my grandpa's door behind me before checking the message.

It's from Chad:

> You never told me if it's okay if I stop by tonight.

I text back with apologies—busy and all that.

> Of course, you can stop by anytime (you don't need permission) and I can't wait to see your surprise.

Back in the Hornet on my way to do errands, I realize it's almost three o'clock. I haven't thought about 758 or its occupant once today.

But I do now.

Chapter | 19

Almost as if external forces are conspiring, I run into Jake again. Well, not really run into, but I catch a glimpse of him pushing a shopping cart in an aisle that I'm walking by. We live in a smallish town, so it's possible Jake's path has crossed mine on other occasions before we knew each other. But unlike our small town, this supermarket is huge, so I think I can avoid him if I hurry and get out of here. He's wearing a red shirt which makes him easy to spot out of the corner of my eye if I need to pretend I don't see him.

But today, fate has it that we both round the corner of the same aisle at the same time. There's no way to turn back without looking like idiots, so we play a game of chicken, both of us pushing our cart forward to the ultimate place where we'll meet.

"Hey," he says when we finally meet. "What's up? How're you doing?"

His smile is so natural I almost believe he's happy to see me.

"I'm doing good," I say. "Busy. How's your summer going?"

"I'm busy too—work, practice. I got out to Santa Cruz last weekend and did some surfing." I wonder if he does the shopping for his family like I do for mine.

The summer is changing him. Even though it hasn't been that long, he seems leaner, his skin darker, his thick, wavy hair longer and lighter. I notice for the first time his eyes are minty green.

"Good. That sounds like fun." My words sound stupid and insipid to me, which makes me wonder what they sound like to Jake.

"Hey, you still living in that tent on the roof?" His grin forces the dimples just where I remember them.

"Yeah, I am." I truly want to spare him from any more small talk. I'm positive he can't wait to get away. "Well, I guess I better get going."

"Okay, see you around. Take care."

I decide a weak smile is a safer answer than anything I could possibly say.

Jake stops to investigate the toothpaste but I can't even remember why I came down this aisle and decide to leave without consulting the rest of the list. I can always come back tomorrow. I make a beeline for the checkout.

While I'm standing in line, I pick up the same celebrity gossip magazine the woman was reading in my father's office. A story on the cover caught my attention earlier today. I thumb through the pages looking for the article when I suddenly feel queasy like I can't trust the ground under my feet. Then I hear a kind of rumbling, and within a few seconds everything is shaking all around me.

I'm a California girl and should be used to earth-quakes, but they always scare me whenever they come. I know right away this is either a big earthquake from far away or a not-so-big one right underneath me. With my heart in a fit of palpitations, I pull my phone from my purse and click on the earthquake app which even-tually confirms it's not a significant earthquake but its epicenter is my town.

Out of the corner of my eye, I see a red shirt approaching. There are a lot of empty checkout counters but Jake comes up right behind me.

"Are you okay?" The concern in his voice sounds genuine.

"Yeah, I'm okay. Just kind of got scared for a minute."

Another sharp jolt rocks the building and I grab onto Jake's arm. This quake is much smaller and shorter in duration. An aftershock.

"Aargh!" I don't want him to know how truly nervous I am right now and I'm embarrassed to have grabbed him like that. "I hate earthquakes."

"I'll walk you to your car. I'm going over to the next checkout. Wait for me." He smiles and then adds, "Good thing you weren't leaning over the edge of your roof when it happened."

Jake helps me unload my bags into the Hornet.

"Do you always do the shopping?" he asks.

"Sometimes. My dad and his girlfriend both work full-time, and on the weekends they try to catch up on stuff. How about you?"

"Me too . . . sometimes. My mom and dad both

work too."

"I started running again." More small talk but hopefully more interesting to him.

"I actually saw you running a few days ago." *So it was him in the Jeep.*

"Yeah, it feels good to be doing something physical since I'm not on swim team this summer."

"You looked pretty good." I know it's a cliché to say his eyes twinkle, but they do. "Running, I mean."

"I saw you yesterday," I say.

"Yeah, I know. I saw you too."

"You didn't say anything—or even wave." We're done looking everywhere but at each other. Now we're looking right into each other's eyes.

"I guess I'm a dick. What's your excuse?" He laughs a little and I laugh too. That massive block of ice, we finally broke through it with an axe.

"Was that your grandfather?"

"It was."

We stare at each other without saying a word. He reaches over and lightly lifts my fingertips with his own, then lets them fall.

"Could we try again?" he asks.

"I'm not very good . . . with guys. I guess I'm a dork. Sorry."

He holds my gaze. "Is that a yes or a no? Just so I know for sure."

"Could we try just being friends?"

He pauses as if he's thinking about something. "I could do that. I could be friends." He gently tucks a strand of loose hair behind my ear and a shiver literally passes down my spine. "So do you want to do something sometime—as friends?"

I hope he's not making fun of me, but it doesn't feel like it.

"I'd like that."

"You still have my number?"

As if I'd ever delete it. "Yeah, I still have it."

"Then shoot me a text sometime . . . if you want."

He turns his shopping cart around and, standing on the back, pushes off with one foot. I watch him ride the cart all the way down the sloped parking lot to his Jeep. Don't know how I didn't see it there when I drove in unless he came after me. He turns around and waves as I'm getting into the car and I wave back. Only then does it occur to me that Grandpa might be at home, scared out of his mind from the earthquake.

When I walk through the front door, Grandpa is waiting.

"Krista, you would not believe what happen to Charlie. I was sleeping soundly, and all of a sudden, this crazy bird start flying around the room flapping his wings and making so much noise, I tell you! It took him five minutes to calm. Then I see your note that you are at the store."

"Did you feel the earthquake?"

"No." He makes a *tsk tsk* noise while shaking his head. "Earthquake?"

"That's probably why Charlie was going nuts. He always freaks when there's an earthquake."

"Ah. This is the reason then."

"Come, Kicsi, let me help you carry the bags and we go have a snack in the kitchen—some cookies from the pretty lady and maybe a nice glass of milk."

"Grandpa, you called me *Kicsi* last night. That was Mom's nickname."

"Yes," he says tenderly. "It means "little one" in Hungarian. Now you are my little one."

"I have to be honest with you . . . it kind of bothers me when you call me that."

"Why, Krista?" Grandpa looks hurt.

"It was Mom's special name, that's all."

"I see . . . then no more Kicsi. Now let's go have some cookies."

MY FATHER AND Marie still aren't home when the doorbell rings. They usually work late on Wednesdays and then stop to pick up dinner on their way home. My grandfather follows me to the front door with the excitement and expectation everyone has when a doorbell rings—even when it's somebody else's home. It's Chad. I'd forgotten all about him.

"Hi, Krista." He's out of breath as though he just ran to the door from his dad's car, which he probably did. "Could you come out on the street for a few minutes? My dad's waiting, and I have to go."

Grandpa follows me out to the street with Chad in the lead. I didn't have time to introduce them, and in fact Chad didn't even seem to notice him. Once we're out on the street, I see Chad's father parked directly opposite my house. His engine is still running. He rolls down the window and waves and I wave back.

"Hope we're not bothering you," he says in a friendly voice. "Chad absolutely had to come show this to you."

"Who is this man and this boy?" my grandfather whispers to me.

"This is my grandpa," I say loudly. Not being sure what to call Chad's dad makes introductions difficult.

"Hi, Krista's grandpa." Chad's father smiles and nods. "I'm Chad's father."

Chad has retrieved a soccer ball from the backseat of the SUV. He looks over at my grandpa as if noticing him for the first time.

"Oh, hi."

My grandpa smiles at each one in turn. He still has no idea who they are even though they now know who he is.

Chad stands in the middle of the street and begins to juggle the ball, counting out loud each time the top of his foot makes contact with the ball.

". . . 23, 24, 25, 26, 27, 28, darn!"

The ball spins off in my grandfather's direction and he catches it on the top of his polished loafer after one bounce. He juggles the ball four or five times without ever touching it with his hand and sends it back to Chad with a perfectly aimed kick.

"Wow," Chad looks at Grandpa with new interest. "You're pretty good."

"Let's go, Chad. We're going to be late. Thanks, Krista. Nice meeting you . . ." Chad's father trails off, not sure what to call my grandpa.

"Great job, Chad! Can't wait to go out with you again. Bye."

I look over at Grandpa who's waving to these two people who are still strangers to him.

"Grandpa, where did you learn to play soccer?"

"Oh, we played all the time when I was little boy. I played with my brothers and all the other kids in my village. But what you call soccer, we call futbol."

"Pretty cool, Grandpa. You haven't lost your skills."

He chuckles. "Who *was* this boy and this man who come and go so quick?"

Chapter | 20

Marie and Dad come home with dinner, and since it's such a nice night, we decide to eat on the back patio. I see the pain in Marie's face when I mention that Chad stopped by for a few minutes and that she just missed him. I didn't want to tell her, but I couldn't exactly keep it from her either—that would have required a conspiracy of at least three people. Chad would have to explain to his mother why he didn't come later when he knew she would be home. But then, Marie probably already knows why. It makes Chad's life easier if he can avoid being in the same place at the same time as both of his parents—even if one of them is waiting in a car, and the other is waiting in a house.

As the light of the day fades, so does Marie. I saw something bleed out of her when she heard about Chad's visit, and she's been unusually quiet ever since then. She's probably still thinking about him and feeling rejected. But, of course, Chad feels rejected by her as well. She rises from her chair and picks up a handful of plates and used napkins which she carries into the kitchen. A few minutes later she comes back and gathers our glasses and empty bottles of sparkling water. Nobody's looking at me to help so I stay where I am. I'm enjoying the velvety night air and the drifting conversation. After her third trip, she doesn't return and since I don't hear any noise in the kitchen, I assume she's gone to bed.

My father is asking my grandfather about the political climate in Venezuela and they're deeply engrossed in the subject but I'm not listening to the words, I'm listening to the mood instead. My grandfather sounds a little sad to me—or maybe he's just tired, which he seems to be a lot. My father sounds wistful—like he's remembering something he misses deeply.

After a while my father excuses himself for the night. He must be aware of Marie's absence by now and he'll either be worried about her or wondering if, somehow, he was the cause of her darkening mood.

But I want Grandpa to myself so I'm secretly relieved when my father leaves. In my hand, I'm holding the ancient picture of him that I found with my mother's notes. I don't know how many opportunities I'll have to bring it up, and since he's in a talkative mood, I decide to go for it.

"Grandpa, I thought you might want to have this." I hold the picture out for him to see.

He takes it in his hand and squints hard while he examines it. Then he sets it face down on the table. I fear that I've made a huge mistake and I hold my breath, unsure of what to say next. The rasping chorus of crickets is loud and grows exponentially in the intensity of our silence. My grandfather reaches over and picks up the picture. He looks at it again and chuckles softly.

"Your mother gives this to you?"

"I found it in her things. There was a journal with some notes she took . . . and a postcard . . . and another note in there too. I thought you might want them."

"No," he sighs. "Better for you to keep." He holds the picture tenderly between his thumb and forefinger. His eyes close, and for a minute, I think he's fallen asleep. "I remember this day."

I know in this moment that Grandpa has given me an opening. And I know that whatever he volunteers, I'll commit to writing tonight in the solitude of my rooftop tent. I'll finish the journal Mom started. The project that was so close to her heart.

"Would you tell me about it?"

IT WOULD TURN out to be a blessing that one of the last truly happy days in the young brothers' lives was captured on camera. Back in those days, in a small village in the Hungarian countryside, photography was rare and expensive, according to Grandpa. But this was a special day—a young couple was to be married and the parents of the bride-to-be had hired a photographer to celebrate the event.

The photographer, a young fellow from the bustling capital city of Budapest, arrived in the village a few days early. In the days leading up to the wedding, he staged various portrait sessions of the townspeople, getting a sense for the light and the local atmosphere. My great-grandparents, hearing this man was in town, scrubbed their four young sons until their skin was practically raw, and then stuffed them into their best formal clothes. They weren't wealthy people so the boys' outfits, by necessity, were passed down from brother to brother. By the time they got to little Vili they were thread-bare and full of telltale patches.

When Grandpa's mother, Helen, found the photographer that day, he was in the middle of staging a session with three older girls and a young mother holding her baby. Who were the girls and the young mother? Grandpa can't remember, but he remembers that no one objected to the last-minute addition of four boys—no one, that is, except the brothers themselves who were allergic to standing still, and anxious to get out of their stiff clothes and back to the serious business of playing.

Using only calm words of encouragement and reassurance, the young photographer stilled his nine subjects and freed the essence of their characters—each and every one of them, on this cool, but sunny, perfectly ordinary autumn day. And as light beams bounced from their hair, faces, arms, jackets, pants, dresses . . . the camera lens methodically collected the rays, directing them back toward the film to create an image that would endure to be seen in a different century on a different continent by a girl who was still less than a dream.

When this moment was over, the boys rushed home to shed their "fine clothes" and change to the far more futbol-friendly outfits they wore nearly every day once their chores and schoolwork were done. On the outskirts of town, they had marked off their soccer field, complete with makeshift goals. They grew up with stories of Gyula Biro, a Jewish Hungarian soccer star who competed in the 1912 Olympics. Biro was only fifteen when he made a national name for himself, and the older boys—Bela and my grandfather—dreamed of following in his footsteps. In a remote Hungarian village, a dream would probably always remain just a dream, but that didn't dampen their enthusiasm.

That day, they were the only boys out on the field, so little Vili and Miklos were relegated to playing goalkeepers to the older brothers, my grandpa and Bela. In practical terms, this meant that the younger brothers chased after a lot of balls. But when the small, dirty faces of a group of Roma boys peered out from behind a cluster of beech trees, a real game suddenly became a possibility. The Romas were gypsies, shunned by most and distrusted by all, but the universal love of sports spoke more powerfully to my grandfather and his three brothers than the warnings of their parents and fellow townspeople.

If the Roma were a clan, well, then my grandpa and his brothers were a clan as well, and when one clan comes up against another, the results are often ugly. History has proved that over and over again and that day would be no different even though, on this perfectly ordinary day, only little boys were involved.

Goals were made, goals were disputed, boys were shoved, unfortunate words were thrown at each other and then, before anyone realized what was happening, the love of the sport had given way to the hatred of intolerance and misunderstanding on both sides.

"What happened next?" I ask my grandpa.

"The oldest Roma boy, he . . . how you say it . . . he put a hex, a curse, on my brothers and on my family. Then they leave and we go home."

The perfectly ordinary day that began in innocence ,memorialized on a strip of celluloid, had ended under an ominous shadow.

A FEW YEARS ago, before the accident, Lyla and I were sitting outside one day talking about what we were going to do that night. It was a warm, breezy, dreamy day—the kind that makes you feel like a little kid. A fly was buzzing somewhere close enough to where I could hear it, and it added to the peace and softness of the moment. I thought about the fly and came to the conclusion that the same fly, buzzing inside my house, would drive me crazy. It would only be a matter of time before I'd look around for a fly swatter or rolled-up newspaper. And yet outside, on that particular kind of a day, it was relaxing.

I thought about it again when, a few days later, I saw a cottontail rabbit before it disappeared into a thicket of brush. On the adorable scale, it ranked high. Aware of my presence it paused momentarily, ears and nose twitching as if to get a fix on how close I was in relation to how quickly it could get to cover. While I watched it, a memory came to me of a rat scurrying through my mother's vegetable garden. The rat had a nose and ears that twitched just like the bunny's nose and ears. In fact, the bunny didn't look all that different from the rat. Its ears were longer, its tail was round instead of long, and it hopped instead of scurried. But otherwise, there wasn't much difference. One animal made me want to reach out to cuddle it; the other filled me with fear and disgust.

I decided then that the human brain might be extremely complex, but in some ways it was unbelievably simple. If I could just succeed in breaking thoughts down to their simplest form, strip them of all senti-ment and cultural bias, I could become the master of my emotions and always make myself happy. Turn every negative into a positive.

The grief that came over me after the accident was like a tidal wave that pinned me to the ocean floor. Helpless against its massive power, I could only wait until it receded and allowed me to surface for a breath. I had to accept that nothing could speed up the process of healing either emotional or physical wounds of this magnitude—a person has to wait for what only time can cure. I would never be clever enough or strong enough to bypass that process.

But tonight, sitting on the roof in my reclining chair, I think about it again. I have hatred in my heart for the man who lives at 758—a man . . . a boy only two years older than me. It came from the same place in my mind where grief and doubt and anger also grew out of absolute numbness. Is there a stem cell for feel-ings? Can we intercept them before they grow out of control . . . or perhaps feed only the ones destined to turn into happiness? Is there a way I can purge myself of hatred once it's taken root? Today was a good day for me. I barely thought about *him* and it felt good to be free of that heavy burden. Of course, it took the violent movement of the ground underneath my feet and Jake's magic dimples to deliver that temporary peace of mind, but still . . .

An owl's golden eyes glow between the leaves of the twisted oak tree. Somewhere on the ground it has spotted the rat that will be its dinner tonight . . . or is it a bunny?

I pick up my phone and type out a text to Jake.

Do you want to run with me tomorrow?

Almost instantly he responds:

How about 7 before I go to work?

Chapter | 21

Thursday morning and I'm up at six. I haven't seen six in the morning for . . . maybe never. But as dumb as it sounds, I want to shower and get ready before my run. I don't want to look like I just fell out of bed when Jake arrives.

Dad's already up, but Marie and Grandpa are still sleeping. Dad is sitting at the kitchen table writing on a sheet of paper which I recognize as my to-do list for the day.

"Krista!" He's surprised to see me at this hour, or even at all. He's usually gone by the time I get up. "Something wrong?"

"No, I just wanted to get in an early run before Grandpa wakes up." I leave out the part about showering and Jake.

"Good for you. I was just making a list for you. Did you mail those things yesterday?"

"No, I'll do it this morning." My father writes "Post Office" on the bottom of the list. "Did Grandpa's test results come back yet?"

"Some of them did. I'm going to have you take him to San Francisco today. A med school friend of mine who teaches there is squeezing him in at three o'clock, so make sure you're early. He's doing me a favor."

"What kind of doctor is he?"

"Hematologist . . . blood."

"What's wrong with Grandpa's blood?"

"Mmmm . . . maybe nothing. They'll be doing a bone marrow test. It's not a big deal but if your grand-father seems nervous you can give him these." He places a tiny envelope in my hand. It contains two round flat yellow pills. "Better have a glass of orange juice and a banana if you're going to run."

I'm WAITING ON the street when Jake pulls up. He gets out of his Jeep and walks over to me. He has sleepy eyes, tousled hair, and looks like he hasn't shaved. I guess he didn't worry like me about making a favor-able early morning impression, but he still looks incred-ible . . . maybe even more than usual.

"Ready?" He smiles brightly.

"I usually do a loop around my neighborhood, and then go down the hill to the place where you saw me that time. There's a tree where I turn around."

"Let's see if we can do better than that today. Maybe we'll motivate each other."

We do some stretches and then start off on a slow jog to warm up.

"Mind if I run behind you?" he smiles slyly. "For the view, that is."

I punch his arm playfully. "Hey!"

"Well I'd rather be in front of you, but it's kind of tough running backward."

As it turns out, I drop behind him in the narrow places where we have to go single file—and I'm the one who gets the great view. What a way to wake up in the morning. Better than that glass of orange juice I had before I left my house. Running with Jake— laughing, talking, sweating together. Like they say in the commercial . . . priceless.

When we get to the turnaround tree, he looks over at me with shoulders shrugged and palms up in a wordless question. I wave my hand forward, I'm not ready to head back yet. We get all the way to town before I realize I may not have the necessary reserves to get home so I swing back toward my house and Jake follows my lead.

I almost make it to the top of the hill, but not quite. My lungs are burning and my legs feel wobbly. Jake turns around and grabs both of my hands. Jogging backward, he half drags me up the rest of the hill. With what little breath I have left, I'm laughing and alter- nating jogging with a sort of lurching Frankenstein walk. I can feel my thin t-shirt clinging to me, soggy with sweat. Jake's face is flushed and shining but he's energetic and could probably do this hill again.

When we get to the top of the hill, there's a narrow walking path sheltered from the sun by a young oak. I pull Jake under its shadow and plunge my fingers into his thick, damp waves of hair, guiding his lips down toward mine in a kiss I never want to end. The sweat trickling into my eyes and the corners of my lips—I'm not sure if its mine or his. He puts his arms behind my back and pulls me even tighter, closer to him. He smells salty and sunny. His kiss tastes like springtime and I melt into his arms, a thousand miles above the earth.

He holds me by my shoulders and pushes me back far enough to look at my face.

"Are we still friends?" he asks. His light-green eyes are unfocused and smoky.

"Wasn't that friendly enough?"

He pulls me back to him and kisses me again, more urgently now, more confident of where we stand.

GRANDPA IS QUIET this morning. I've taken my second shower of the day and it's only eight o'clock—I wasn't in a rush to wash off the memory of my morning run, but I didn't think Grandpa would appreciate sitting down to breakfast with the odor of that memory.

I decide to surprise him with one of the few things I actually do know how to cook—scrambled eggs. They're dry but he eats them politely along with the whole-wheat toast and orange juice, complimenting me all along. There's not a lot of conversation but I can tell he appreciates my effort. After breakfast, he goes up to his room, taking with him a little plate of eggs for Charlie. It seems cannibalistic but I know birds love to eat eggs.

Once I've cleaned up in the kitchen I knock on Grandpa's door and he lets me in, and then quickly closes the door behind me so Charlie doesn't escape. But Charlie looks like he has no intention of ever leaving this man's side. He's perched on the edge of the plate and has almost completely finished the eggs.

"He's a good bird, this Mr. Charlie," my grandfather says thoughtfully. "He steps on my finger last night."

"What? That's great news, Grandpa!" He has said it in such a matter-of-fact way that I realize he doesn't grasp the significance of it.

"You try. He will go to you."

I'm scared to try because I don't want to be rejected by Charlie again, but my grandfather sounds so confident in such a nonchalant way that I feed off his confidence and extend my finger in front of Charlie.

"Push a little," Grandpa encourages me. "He needs to get used to these things."

Following his instructions, I push my finger into Charlie's pink, fleshy chest and he looks up from his scrambled egg breakfast and steps onto my finger, first one foot and then the other. I feel his full weight on my outstretched finger.

We gave Charlie everything we thought he wanted—a quiet room, toys, special seed. Grandpa didn't see the pink, featherless flesh, he just saw a bird, and I guess I'm not much different from the little gray bird that doesn't want to be special. Visible pinfeathers are sprouting from Charlie's bare chest.

Chapter | 22

I never spent much time in doctors' offices, because I had a doctor at home, and no matter what was wrong, my dad would usually tell me that I would get better, and I always did. I guess he instilled in me a sense that complaining was self-indulgent and weak—that I should suck it up and be strong when faced with sickness or adversity. Mom was nurturing—completely the opposite of Dad. If any of us was ever sick, Mom was there with hot tea, soup, comforting words. But I must have more of Dad's genes because I tend to hold things in just like he does—or at least I try.

The hematologist's office in this university medical center is a depressing place. People seem defeated and scared. Shoulders are hunched over months-old magazines that have been paged through so many times they're creased like an old man's face. People look fearfully toward the door every time the nurse opens it to call for the next patient—as though she's the escort to an underworld from which there's no escape.

Once my grandfather has been called, and I'm left alone to wait for him, I become one of the healthy attending people. But most of the healthy attending people accompany the patients behind the door—husbands and wives who will share in the pain of their mates. I feel like I get more than my fair share of glances from the others after my grandpa gets up—as if they're feeding off my youth and good health. As if I remind them of what they once were before whatever it was that brought them to this sad place. But that might just be my imagination and have more to do with my own insecurities about being here with Grandpa. I want him to be anywhere else but here—even safely back in Venezuela before I knew him in a way that made me care so much.

Lyla is the perfect antidote to this waiting room, and she's been texting me for the past ten minutes. Faster than I can type a reply, she out-texts me two to one. She's on a high, in a love fog over some boy she's met at the beach. I know more about him in ten minutes than his parents probably learned in his life-time. But I can't bring myself to tell her about Jake. It still seems so new and fragile and I want to protect it. I'm not even sure where it's going after this morning. He'll be leaving for football camp in a few days and that will give us both a week away from each other. A week when he'll be too busy to think about me during the day and too tired to think about me at night. I, on the other hand, will be thinking about him night and day. And even as I think about him now, a text arrives, inter-rupting Lyla's nonstop stream.

Jake:

What are you wearing?

Me:

Ha ha. I'm sitting in a doctor's office waiting for my grandpa.

Jake:

Can't blame me for fantasizing. He okay?

Me:

Ya, I think so.

We make plans to get together tomorrow night. He's leaving in two days for football camp.

I'm the only one left in the waiting room by the time Grandpa comes out. I've been here for over two hours and have read every magazine on the messy table in front of me—even *Field and Stream*. Lyla moved on to other things long ago. I even tried to text Chad but got no response.

Grandpa says the biopsy didn't really hurt, but the site is tender, and he's limping a little. I know what kind of traffic we're facing this time of day heading out of San Francisco. We talk it over and decide it would be best to have dinner here and go home once the traffic dies down. It's easy to pick a place—we both love Chinese food and we're not too far from Chinatown.

"Did the doctor tell you when you'll get the results?"

"He says he will call your father. He knows I visit only for a short time."

I haven't thought about Grandpa as visiting for a short time or leaving soon—I've already incorporated him into my life. He plumps up my family which used to be bigger and now feels precariously small.

"How long, Grandpa . . . before you leave?"

"I have my ticket only for one week. I go back on Tuesday, unless . . . unless . . ."

I DRIVE INTO the parking garage and spiral down further and further until I finally find an open space. It's dark and stuffy down here, like a dungeon. We cram into a tiny elevator where we're wedged shoulder to shoulder—or shoulder to hip in the case of the young boy by my side. His mother puts a reassuring hand on the side of his head and he dips instinctively toward her. It makes me think of the photo where my grandpa leans protectively into little Vili. The clipped, sharp sounds of Mandarin pass back and forth between a white-haired man and his tiny, stooped wife who stand behind me. The elevator shudders and lurches as it makes its way out of this pit of darkness. My grandpa looks over at me and shrugs, a half-smile on his face. If an earthquake is in my future, I only hope it waits until the elevator doors open above the ground.

Out in the street it's like we've entered a new country—China! We walk through narrow alleys and wide roads. Like a river, there's a flow of humans moving along the sidewalks. Everyone looks like they have someplace to get to and not very much time to get there. We pass by little shops with jade figurines, delicate porcelain tea cups, and silk robes enticingly displayed in the windows. Naked ducks hang upside down under pink heating lamps in a marketplace where buckets full of gray fish slap against each other inside their cylindrical prison walls.

A man with translucent skin partially covered by patches of wispy white whiskers shuffles along. His eyes are blue with blindness, but his progress forward is steady and sure. Pedestrians approaching him from behind peel away on either side of him, creating a perpetual halo of cement around him. He stops as if to take a breath, and with great effort, he brings a ball of phlegm from his throat into his mouth where he shoots it in the direction of the gutter, narrowly missing a passerby. I glance at a pair of embroidered, black velvet flats in the window of one store for just a few seconds too long. Grandpa follows my gaze and insists that we go inside the store to buy them.

These streets are hilly and difficult to navigate. I worry about Grandpa who looks pale and tired. His limp is becoming more pronounced.

"This looks like a good place," I suggest just because we happen to be standing right in front of it. "Shall we go in?"

The restaurant is small and there is no pretense of décor or ambience. Formica tables, stained yellow over the years, are functional, as are the blue molded-plastic chairs. The table is badly out of balance, so I fold up a napkin and slide it under the wobbling leg. A surly waiter walks by, and without so much as a backward look, he sets down two laminated menus. He comes back only minutes later for our order, which, fortunately, we're prepared to give. A jumbo-sized plastic bottle of soda adorns every table. The waiter opens ours and pours out two glasses which we haven't requested but nevertheless pick up to drink.

I pull the wooden chopsticks from their paper sleeve and force them apart until they snap into two separate sticks. Grandpa carefully unfolds his paper napkin and tucks it into the top of his shirt.

"What happened to the gypsy boys after they put a curse on your family? Did you ever see them after that?" The look on his face makes me quickly add, "We don't have to talk about it if you don't want to."

"I tell you the story, Kicsi." I decide not to protest his use of this endearment anymore. It might sting momentarily but it must bring him some comfort or he wouldn't revert to it. "I tell you because it's more important for you to remember than for me to forget." As if something else is bothering him, he looks down at his hands that are folded and resting on the table. "And because I never tell your mother when she ask." He speaks in a voice that is barely audible above the clatter of dishes in the kitchen.

And now I know that Grandpa has given me permission to finish Mom's journal.

THINGS WENT DOWNHILL quickly after that day, Grandpa said. The Jewish population in Grandpa's village was about twenty percent, and new regulations required them to wear a large yellow star sewed onto their clothing when they went out in public. Grandpa said he hadn't felt any different from the other children in the village until then, even though most of them were Christians. They had played together and gone to the same school. They worshipped separately, but that felt natural—as natural as when boys and girls separated for various activities. But soon the yellow star felt like a scalding brand which seared the skin on his chest, and he felt ashamed for being different without even knowing why.

One day Hungarian soldiers showed up in town and when they left, my great-grandfather, Jeno, left with them. Just like that . . . no time for goodbyes or to settle any affairs, just time enough to pack a small bag with a few clothes and all the food his wife could get her hands on. Other Jewish fathers, husbands, and older brothers left with him. They were going to work for the state, they were told. They were going to be part of the war effort.

When he took his seat in the back of a large military truck, he looked around anxiously for his wife and sons. As the convoy pulled out of the village, he waved and called out for them to obey their mother and take care of each other. He would write to them when he got a chance. He would be back soon. A million kisses.

Did he know this was the last time they would lay eyes on each other? Probably not, he admitted. We never know what our future holds, and even though we all know that death is a certainty, we persevere in the face of it, mock it, and live in denial of it—the human condition is what they call that.

With husbands and fathers gone, households struggled to carry on. Jeno was a mover. He owned a horse and carriage, and he moved people from house to house and village to village. He relied on the strength of his back and his sturdy horse. His boys were only just beginning to be old enough to be useful in the business. But now with their father gone, Bela and his mother attempted to carry on. My grandfather at ten years old pitched in as well. The two younger brothers did what they could.

Christian friends and neighbors, with whom they had

lived harmoniously, were sympathetic at first, but as time went on, they began to withdraw—perhaps fearing for their own safety, should they be accused of helping the Jews; perhaps they were beginning to believe the hateful propaganda that spread its vile tentacles into the poisoned Hungarian earth. Regardless of the reason, business dwindled to almost nothing and Helen was nearing the end of her family's resources, having sold anything of value long ago.

Two people who did not turn their backs on Helen and the boys were the Barnas. An older, childless couple, they often paid young Gyuri, my grandpa, to do chores around their property. They raised chickens and kept a milk cow, so Gyuri was usually sent home with a small cloth bundle into which Agnes Barna tied up eggs and cheese. Having no children of their own, the Barnas showered my grandpa with affection and attention. Agnes frequently sat with him at the kitchen table going over his schoolwork, giving him the one-on-one attention it was impossible to get in a family of four boys.

Sometime in the early months of 1944, Jeno sent the postcard that would rest in my hands seventy years later. There had been other cards from him before he reached Buchenwald, but this was the one fate would select to survive.

T.S. Eliot said that April was the cruelest month, but in Hungary in 1944 that distinction belonged to May. The deportation of the Jewish population would begin on the 15th day of that month, and in the next three months, even though it was clear that Germany was losing the war, nearly half a million Hungarian Jews would systematically be deported and murdered. Winston Churchill would later call the persecution and deportation of the Hungarian Jews the "greatest and most horrible crime ever committed in the whole history of the world."

But in the weeks leading up to it, my grandpa still had to go about the business of being a ten-year-old boy. Sometimes, even in those desperate days, that meant disobeying your mother, who didn't have the benefit of a husband to back her up in matters of disciplining four free-spirited young boys. That sometimes meant playing when you should be working. And sometimes it meant being out after dark when you were supposed to be in bed.

On one particular day, it meant sneaking off to the Barnas when you were supposed to be at home writing another unanswered letter to your father who hadn't been heard from in months. Grandpa was hungry and there were always good things to eat at the Barnas. He would bring something home for his mother and brothers like he always did, and Helen would soon forget that she was ever angry at his disobedience. Anyhow, she never really got angry anymore—she seemed to be slowly giving up. The truth was, if the Barnas had the time for Gyuri, she was grateful because she was running out of reserves of time and inner strength.

But on this particular day that should have been a lovely spring day in the Hungarian countryside, the soldiers came for the Jewish families that were still left in Gyuri's village. For Helen, Bela, Miklos, and Vili, they would begin their journey on this day, first by truck, then by train, to the camp on the outskirts of the Polish town, Oświęcim—an extermination camp that the Nazis called Auschwitz, and whose name would soon become synonymous with Evil itself.

Weeks later, when Agnes Barna slipped into my grandpa's vacant family home, she found the postcard from Jeno still lying on the kitchen table. Perhaps in her haste Helen left it behind, although Grandpa never doubted she purposely left it for him. And right next to the postcard, on the rough wooden *table, was the picture of four smiling brothers taken on that perfectly ordinary day in a different time and a different world that would never again be the same.*

. . . a million kisses . . .

Chapter | 23

By the time Grandpa and I are home, it's dark, and I'm surprised to see Emma and Chad are here. They run to open the door when they hear the key in the lock.

"Hi Krista!" Emma hugs my legs. She's dressed in light blue cotton pajamas dotted with yellow daisies. "Guess what?"

"We're going to Disneyland," Chad blurts out.

"Cha-ad! No fair, Mommy said I could tell Krista."

Chad pulls out his cell phone and flips through his pictures before stopping and clicking on one.

"Look!" He beams proudly. "thirty-three." A tiny Chad juggles a soccer ball across the screen of his phone.

"I took the video, Krista!" Emma fights to reclaim the attention.

My grandfather smiles and looks from Emma to Chad and back to Emma again. "Very good. Nice work. Very good," he says before disappearing into his room.

He has an easy way of making sense out of nonsense.

"Where's Charlie, Krista?" Emma knows if she keeps talking Chad will eventually give up and leave the stage to her. "I looked for him and I couldn't find him."

I haven't been able to do anything more than grunt since I walked in the door but nobody seems to notice or care.

"He's in my grandpa's room. He's been staying there the last few days," I finally get a word in.

"That's your grandpa, Krista?" Emma is wide-eyed. "He's old."

"Not really. Remember, I'm a lot older than you are." I'm a little confused . . . and surprised by their unexpected appearance. "Who's going to Disneyland and when are you going?"

"Mom's taking us," Chad beats Emma to this answer. "Just the three of us. We're leaving tomorrow morning . . . can you drive us to the airport?"

"Sure." I'm still puzzled, although some pieces are falling together. It seems Marie wants to reconnect with her kids after Chad's unannounced visit. I know that sometimes even little things can lead to big changes. "I'm happy for you guys. You'll have a great time!"

I DROP MARIE and the kids at the airport, still a little confused about the whole situation, including why Dad didn't take them himself. I'm guessing it had to do with work but I thought I detected a stillness in the air between them. They were polite toward each other all morning—maybe too polite—and they even hugged and kissed before Marie got in the car. But something had changed, that much I knew.

Dad is gone by the time I get back, and Grandpa is watching the Spanish channel on TV. I wonder if he knows something that I don't, but even if he does, I don't think he'd say.

"Do you miss Venezuela?" I startle him. He didn't know I was back.

"No, no." He seems embarrassed to be caught watching TV and quickly turns it off. "What is our plan today? Where is your list?"

Dad has left the list on the kitchen counter. No doctors' appointments today. Just a few simple tasks—pay the gardener when he comes, pick up some office supplies at the store. I guess my day is free for the most part.

"What would you like to do today, Grandpa? It's a wide-open day."

Tonight, I'll be getting together with Jake but only for a short time. He has to go to bed early because he leaves for football camp at six tomorrow morning.

"We could drive somewhere? Have some lunch later?"

"Okay. Where would you like to drive?"

"You decide, Kicsi. Somewhere nice and pretty. Maybe the ocean or a lake if it isn't too far."

"Do you mind if I take a quick run—thirty minutes max?"

"You take all the time you want. I'm not in hurry. Me and Mr. Charlie, we will find something to do."

Now that I've started, I don't want to miss a single day of running. If it's an obsession, at least it's a healthy one, and I've invented a sort of game or mantra to go along with it. Every time my foot hits the ground I imagine a puff of stress shooting out of my ear. And every time I lift my foot from the ground, I imagine sucking the strength of the earth through my shoe, up my leg, and straight into my lungs. The music from my earbuds is the fuel that keeps me going.

I'm almost home when Rachel flags me down. She's outside watering her flowers and Henry's nowhere to be seen. She waves me over.

"Come inside, I've got some cookies I just baked for you and your grandfather. I know he likes them."

I follow her into the house.

"I'm kind of sweaty." I wipe my forehead with the back of my arm.

"That's okay. Can you stay for a few minutes? Henry's sleeping."

I can hear the baby monitor hissing in the kitchen.

"I have a white noise machine on in his room," she explains.

Rachel peels the cookies off the pan with a spatula and lays them on a thick paper plate. I can tell they're still warm because they bend to fit the curvature of the plate. A rustling sound comes over the monitor and Rachel freezes. When the sound stops, she returns to prying off cookies.

The absolute parent-child connection astonishes me. Totally giving up your independence to listen to the sounds of a sleeping baby—who would volunteer for that? What happens to grown-ups that makes them crave this lifestyle?

"How are you doing, Krista?"

I hesitate for just a moment. I want to tell someone

about Jake, but other than Lyla, who is there to tell?

"I have a boyfriend . . . sort of."

Rachel looks up at me with surprise. I don't know if she's happy or shocked.

"That's wonderful. Who is he?"

"His name is Jake Robbins. We go to school together."

"Robbins . . . is that Robbins Electric?"

"Yeah, that's his dad."

"His father is a nice man. He did some work for us last year."

Jake's dad was right next door to me last year. But why would I have noticed . . . or cared at the time?

"Are you ready for this, Krista?"

"For a boyfriend? I think so. Why shouldn't I be?"

"You want to be in a good place when you're in a relationship. You want to be able to share things with each other . . . and make sure he treats you respectfully."

"He does." I laugh even though she hasn't said anything funny. I guess I'm a little nervous.

"Well, I'm here for you—you know that. If you want to talk about him or anything else." She looks at me meaningfully. "You know we've never really talked about what happened."

"I don't need to . . . do that."

Now I'm sorry I brought up Jake. I didn't expect this reaction. I thought Rachel, of all people, would be happy for me.

"Krista, you can trust me with your feelings. I share them and I want to protect you. I feel like I've lost both a sister and a daughter. I understand, I really do."

A tear slides down her cheek. She cradles my face

gently with one hand, but feeling me flinch, she withdraws quickly. The cookies are piled high on the plate and loosely covered with aluminum foil. Rachel hands the plate to me.

"Thanks, Rachel. Grandpa will love them, but I better get home."

She looks at me seriously. "Please. You can't shoulder this by yourself. If not me, then maybe Dr. Bronstein."

"You've been talking to my dad," I say, feeling betrayed by him once again.

"Your father loves you. I love you."

The plate of cookies feels like a heavy weight in my hand. Rachel has ruined my high. Thinking about Dr. Bronstein makes me feel bad again. Nobody believes in me except . . . maybe Grandpa.

Grandpa. I'm anxious for him to finish his story. I need to hear the rest of it and write it down before he goes away.

"I have to get going. My grandpa and I have plans," I say.

She hugs me with one arm and I give her a half-hearted peck on the cheek.

Cooing and gurgling baby noises float out of the monitor. The invisible string pulls Rachel back to Henry's room.

Chapter | 24

Grandpa and I load up on picnic food at a Russian deli in town. It's the closest thing to a Hungarian Jewish deli that I can offer him. Afterward, I'm tempted to drive to the ocean, one of his requests and the one I sense he would most like, but I'm worried about getting back in time for Jake, so we go to the Reservoir instead.

I spread a thick woolen blanket underneath the shade of a tree with pointy lime-green leaves that remind me of butterfly wings in the breeze.

"Your father talk to me this morning when you gone. He have test results from my . . ."

"Biopsy?" Now I know why my father stayed behind instead of driving Marie to the airport.

"Biopsy, yes."

"And?"

"There are some cells in my bone marrow that look funny . . . I can't remember how it's called. My body doesn't make enough of the red cells anymore. This is why I am tired and peel."

"Is it serious?"

"No, I don't think so. Anyway, life is serious."

"What's the treatment for it?"

"I think I will get some blood transfusion. And then some kind of vitamin and medicine. I will find a doctor . . . a hematologist when I go back to Venezuela."

"I wish you wouldn't leave, Grandpa. I wish you'd stay and live with us."

"I will come back soon, but I have things to do before I get old, you understand." He chuckles.

"I'm sorry, Grandpa. About your disease."

He makes a *tsk* sound with the tip of his tongue and shakes his head.

"Don't be sorry. I have good luck my whole life . . . so now I have a little bad luck, that's all."

"Do you believe you've had good luck?"

"Yes, of course. When others die, I live. So I'm a lucky man."

"Did you ever see the gypsy boy again?"

IT WASN'T SAFE to stay in the village after that day, Grandpa said, but the Barnas hid young Gyuri in their barn for the next few months until life returned to normal, or what would become the new normal of the time. The day after Helen and the boys were taken away, Mr. Barna went to their home to fetch the horse. He answered the curious stares of neighbors when they saw him harnessing the horse to the cart by explaining that Helen had obligations to him and this would settle her debts. That seemed to satisfy everyone. Within a few weeks, all of Helen and Jeno's remaining belongings would be pilfered by their former friends and neighbors. And the Barnas had an urgent need for the horse and moving cart.

Months later, Mr. Barna harnessed the horse to the cart once again and set out to visit a cousin in a nearby village. The cart was loaded with old furniture that would be reupholstered and refinished by his cousin for resale purposes—at least this was the explanation given to the Barnas' nosy neighbor who was unaware that young Gyuri had been hiding for months in the barn only a few hundred yards from her home. Twisting his body to fit underneath the various legs of the chairs, my grandfather lay with his tender young cheek pressed hard against the rough wood of the bottom of the cart. Had anyone been suspicious enough to lift the protective tarp from the top of the chairs, both young Gyuri and old Mr. Barna would have met the same cruel fate.

The journey didn't end in the nearby village—that was only the beginning. From there my grandfather was moved along from stranger to stranger—people willing to risk their lives rather than turn their backs on civilization and humanity.

After some months, he found himself in the capital city of Budapest, which was elegantly draped along both banks of the Danube River. The stately beauty of the city hid its most vile secret—a walled ghetto that served as a massive prison for seventy thousand of Budapest's remaining Jewish citizens. Within these walls, people lived like filthy animals—food was not allowed in, garbage was not collected, rats scurried brazenly down sidewalks where raw sewage flowed alongside the curbs. Typhoid and hunger claimed life after life, leaving behind corpses to be tossed like peanut shells into vast pits that served as mass graves.

My grandfather was a lucky boy but he didn't feel that way. Were you lucky if your whole family was dead but you were still alive? If he hadn't disobeyed his mother, he would be dead too. And many times, he thought that's exactly what should have happened.

Until the Russians liberated Hungary, he posed as a doctor's assistant—a young lad from the countryside who worked to help his family out financially. After the war ended, he stayed on with the doctor and his wife, who housed him and fed him and taught him the art of healing during the days, and the stuff of schoolboys at night.

But as kindly and well-meaning as they were, they didn't have the medicine to heal his heart, and so that cancer of hate ate away at him day by day, month by month, and finally year by year. At the age of seventeen, after several close calls with the Russian soldiers who became Hungary's newest cruel masters, the doctor and his wife encouraged my grandpa to leave. Not just the city, but to leave Hungary behind forever and make a new start in a place where he had a chance at happiness, a chance of forgetting.

There was one final thing that Gyuri, a young strapping man, had to do. He returned to his village which by now was unrecognizable to him. Not a single Jew had returned, probably none had survived. Strangers now lived in his old family home. His homecoming with the Barnas was bittersweet. He loved them for what they had risked for his sake—but he knew he would never see them again once he left. He spent a few months with them, making plans for how he would escape from Hungary, which had become a giant prison behind the wall of the Iron Curtain. And then a few days before he left, he went to the place where he knew the gypsies of his childhood had lived in a more or less permanent camp-

site.

He knew the Roma boy was not capable of causing death and devastation through a childish hex. He didn't truly believe in curses even when he was a young boy of ten. And yet, for some reason, he couldn't completely shake the episode from his mind—it was always with him, like a headache you wake up with every morning and go to bed with every night.

This day, when he went to find the gypsy boy who would now be a young man himself, he found, as he suspected, nobody . . . and nothing. Just like the Jews, the Roma had vanished—erased from the landscape by the Nazis. Right then and there, my grandfather realized he hadn't come to this place looking for revenge; he had come hoping to find life.

"DO YOU STILL think about your family, Grandpa?"

"Every day." He leans back on one elbow and looks out at the glittering blue water where white pelicans float into each other like bumper boats in an amusement park. "I think about them every day. You? Do you think about your family?"

I start to say I miss my family, but the word sticks in my throat. Miss? I miss Lyla. Next week I'll miss Jake until he gets back. But I'm going to see them both at some point. Miss doesn't seem to be the right word. And because I can't find the right word, I just nod my head.

"Do you still hate them? The Nazis?"

He doesn't answer right away. He looks like he's thinking hard about this question and about his answer. As though he's never considered it before, although I know he has a thousand times.

"I couldn't hate everyone—there were too many to hate. Where would I stop? Hate doesn't hurt the hated person . . . it only hurts the person who hates."

"I wanted to go back to see the boy—Omar Aziz." I can't believe I've said his name out loud, maybe for the first time. "But everyone stopped me. Everyone made me feel bad about myself for wanting to do that."

"I think you should go see him, Kicsi," my grandfather says quietly.

"What would I say?"

"You will know what to say . . . but don't go with hate in your heart."

Chapter | 25

I'm disappointed when Jake calls to tell me he's going to be late. Something about an emergency job that came in for his father, and he has to help because his dad couldn't round up an assistant in time. It means extra money for the family because it came in after regular business hours, so they can charge more.

Dad is also working after regular business hours. He was called in tonight to admit one of his patients to the hospital. Dad traded with his partner to be on call this weekend since Marie is out of town. So it's just Grandpa and me for dinner.

We get Chinese take-out of course. Then we play with Charlie for a while and my grandpa gets an idea.

"Let him fly around the house," he suggests.

Which we do. Charlie finds a place on top of the curtain rod in the living room, and he's probably making quite a bird mess up there, but we don't care. We're just happy to see him happy. And the pink flesh of his chest is beginning to look like a pin cushion full of little spikes that will soon unfurl into brand new real feathers.

We sit outside in the darkness and I pull my hair away from my face and fasten it into a ponytail. The warm, cozy breeze tickles the back of my neck and shoulders. I think about Jake and am so filled with anticipation that my stomach has flutters. I think about what Grandpa said earlier and the anticipation turns to dread. I'm on a rollercoaster for sure.

Grandpa looks up in the sky at the smoothly gliding owl that has just passed overhead. Then his attention turns to the stars.

"So many stars. In the old days, people used the stars to guide their way at night. When I left my beautiful Hungary, I used them too."

Our night sky is all the more dramatic with no street or city lights to compete.

"Millions . . ." he says softly.

BY THE TIME Jake arrives, Grandpa has already turned in for the night, and even Dad is back from the hospital and in bed reading. I go into Dad's room to say goodnight, but he's sound asleep, glasses still on and the book laying on the floor by the side of his bed. I turn off his light and carefully remove the glasses from his face. He mumbles something and turns over on his side, snoring within seconds. My heart fills with a love for him I haven't felt for a long time.

I'm doing everything I can to distract myself when I hear a quiet knock at the front door. I'm so excited that he's here, it almost feels like I'm flying on winged feet. But then the sad part. It's really late and Jake still hasn't had a chance to pack for his week-long trip. He only has an hour—sorry about that.

So we only have an hour; that's better than nothing—what shall we do? After snuggling and kissing and breathing tickly whispers into each other's ears about how much we missed the other, I have a thought.

"Let's do speed dating."

Jake smiles and shakes his head. "Whatever you say. You're the boss tonight."

We go up to the tent for privacy, just in case my dad or grandpa happens to wake. We crawl inside and lie down with our heads near the opening so we can look up at the sky, and we hold each other.

"So, what's speed dating?" he asks, his lips a fraction of an inch from mine.

"Well . . . what do we really know about each other? We get to ask each other questions."

"You first. I know everything I need to know." He pulls me closer to him.

There's so much I don't know about him that I can't think where to start.

"What's your middle name?"

"Everett. What's yours?"

"Helene. Um . . . How many girlfriends have you had?"

"Whoa!" Jake laughs and pulls back to look at me. "This is speed dating?"

"You have to answer."

"Okay . . . two. No, three." My heart sinks. "But one

of them was in second grade and another only lasted two weeks."

"How about the third?"

"One of those summer camp kind of things. I wouldn't technically call her a girlfriend. Okay, how about you?"

"None. Just you . . . that is . . . if you're my boyfriend." I'm glad it's dark because I know my cheeks are burning bright red.

"I want to be." His eyes defocus like that first time he kissed me, and he kisses me again.

I'm tingling inside so much it's like someone filled me up with peppermint oil, but I pull myself together. Our time is running out. Time. It's not dependable. It can't be relied upon. I have a sudden urge to come completely clean with Jake but, of course, I can't. He'd run away so fast before I ever had the time to really know him. And time is what I need and want the most.

"What's your favorite food? And then you have to come up with the next question instead of just repeating mine."

"Pizza. Okay . . . let's see." He pretends to look deep in thought, but I know he's exhausted.

"What was your worst day ever?" He scrunches his face so tight his eyes shut. "Sorry. I'm an idiot. Uh . . . What do you want to be?" I should get used to questions like that if I plan on rejoining the world. I squeeze his hand to let him know it's alright and give myself a virtual pat on the back for being able to handle it.

"A famous author. How about you?"

"The starting quarterback of the 49ers," he laughs.

"Do you know I've never been to a football game before? But I'll definitely go watch you play."

"Do you know I've never read a book that hasn't been assigned by a teacher? But I'll read yours when you write one."

We know a little bit more about each other, but Jake has to leave. He leaves me with more kisses and promises to text.

Our time has come to an end.

AFTER JAKE LEAVES, I'm so wound up that I can't sleep. I want to call him or text him but it's already midnight and he hasn't packed. He'll only get a few hours of sleep tonight so I can't do that to him. I feel like I'm ready to tell Lyla about Jake but it's three in the morning where she is. I can't focus on a book or TV. This is what I get for basically having only one friend— two now with Jake. And maybe Chad counts for a half because we have an understanding but he's too young to talk to about important things.

I think about how Mom would drive me around at night when I couldn't sleep. Right now, I wish I had someone to drive me somewhere, but I can still drive myself. And once I'm in the Hornet, the car seems to drive itself . . . straight to 758.

I know I'm not going to talk to Omar. That's not the point tonight. What is the point then? Maybe a dry run. I'm going to do it sooner rather than later. Grandpa said not to go with hate in my heart and this is the closest I've come to that state of mind in two years. The timing seems to be now or never. Tomorrow. I'll do it tomorrow.

I roll down all the windows and crank up the music, and when I'm driving on the freeway I feel brave and strong and capable of anything. The wind rushes through one side of the car and out the other, and I'm caught up in a vortex of adrenaline.

But as soon as I signal to get off the freeway at the exit which will lead me to 758, my confidence drains like a pin-pricked water balloon. By the time I'm cruising through the streets I feel shaky inside and I wonder what madness brought me to this area at this time of night. Every house I pass seems to shout out at me.

Go home! Leave us alone! You don't belong here!

And finally, I'm at the street where I make a right that leads me to the house. But it's dark and I'm not going to stop. I know that. I knew it before I came here. I just want to see the car. His car. I want to be prepared for tomorrow. Or if not tomorrow, when the time is right. Time.

The brown Toyota with the silver patches is in the driveway and its door is open. The interior light illuminates the dark silhouette of a man who has his left foot on the driveway and his right foot still in the car. He's either just coming or just leaving, and at the exact moment I drive by, his head swivels and our eyes connect.

I keep driving without slowing down and I make two rights to avoid having to make a U-turn and go by the house again. But by the time I've come to the end of the block that would take me back to El Dorado and eventually the freeway, I can see the brown Toyota in my rear-view mirror.

At this late hour, the stoplights on El Dorado are timed to stay green most of the time, so fortunately I don't have to come to a stop. But every time I look in the mirror, he's still behind me. My hands are shaking, so I grip my steering wheel harder but that does nothing for my heart, which feels like a fish flopping around in an inch of water. I'm scared and I want to call someone, but who? 9-1-1? They'd probably arrest *me*! When I finally reach the freeway entrance, I press down hard on the accelerator to merge into traffic.

But the brown Toyota is still behind me. I move over a lane and it moves over too. I pull all the way over to the fast lane on the left and it follows my lead as though we're connected by an invisible tow line. At the last minute, just before my freeway exit, I change lanes quickly to the right and exit, not daring to look behind me.

At the bottom of the off-ramp, there's a stop sign. I breathe a deep sigh of relief and then look in my rear-view mirror. And he's behind me . . . waiting for my next move. I have no choice but to go home. Where else can I go? At least Dad and Grandpa are there and can help me. But help me with what? What's he going to do to me?

There's no point in driving fast now; I'm not going to lose him. This is what it's all come down to, what I wanted—isn't it? I try to stay calm in order to face the inevitable. I breathe slowly and deeply. I've set this into motion, and now I have to deal with it. How much worse can it be? How much worse can my life get? As I drive up the steep hill to cover the final distance before my house, I slow down slightly to give him a chance to keep up.

And then we both park our cars in front of my house. We're on opposite sides of the street and it takes me a minute to work up the nerve to open my door. His door opens right away and he steps out of his car but doesn't move toward me. He just leans against his car. He's tall and slender like my dad. By the light of the night sky, I can make out that his hair and eyes are dark. He turns his head slightly and the shadows that fall over it reveal a sculpted nose and jawline. I'm so detached at this moment, I'm almost robotic. My breaths continue to come slow and easy. I can handle this by myself. I'm strong. Dr. Bronstein never prepared me for this moment. Never could. But my heart pounds so heavily, so incongruously to my detached resolve that I'm confused for a few seconds before I return to the place where I am that coldly calculating girl again.

Do it.

He's wearing a uniform of some sort—maybe he's a waiter, or even a busboy in a nice restaurant. I stare directly at him and he drops his eyes. I wonder . . . if I saw this man in a restaurant and he was bussing my table, would I ever wonder about his life—who he was going home to, who he loved, who he hated? Would I even see him at all?

I press myself against the door of the Hornet for the false security it provides. The time has come for me to say what I need to say. Time. But my vocal cords seem absolutely paralyzed. I have the feeling that if I attempt to speak, I might physically choke on my own words.

"Is this what you want?" he says finally in a slightly

accented voice. "Do you want to see me? See the monster? Here I am, then."

This is it. This is the moment. What do I say, Grandpa?

"Say whatever you want to me. Do whatever you want. I don't care. But please leave my mother and my brother and sister in peace. They've done nothing. They're innocent and have already suffered enough because of me."

What do I say, Grandpa?

"I have to take care of them—you understand? There's nobody else but me. So say it. Hit me. Do what you will. I don't care!"

I can hear the sob coming up his throat well before it turns into a sound. He buries his face into his hands and says something I can't hear or maybe don't understand. Then he looks up at me and his eyes, even at this distance, are like black holes swallowing all the pain in the world.

"I think about them every day," he says. "Both of them, but especially your sister. I went to her and she looked up at me. I tried to help her. I tried . . . and I couldn't do anything to save her. They pushed me away. I tried . . . but I couldn't do anything . . . I couldn't do anything for her." Deep, wretched sobs escape from his chest, and a light comes on in the Sullivans' second floor window.

I simply fade away into the depths of his pain. Is this the peace I wanted? Is this the resolution I was seeking at 758?

Or is this what it feels like to die?

I get into my car and drive away from his words.

And from my absolute lack of words.

Chapter | 26

In a front window of Jake's house, I see the tell-tale flickering blue light of a late-night television. Two faces appear in the scallop-shaped glass window at the top of the door in response to my knock.

"I'll get it, Tyler," a woman's voice says. I can see her face, blurred slightly by the beveled glass.

A porch light comes on and the door opens, just barely.

"Is Jake home?" I see my pitiful reflection in the expression on his mother's face.

"Are you . . . Krista?" She opens the door fully and stands aside for me to enter.

"Yes." My voice is so small I can hardly hear it myself.

"Mom! What if it wasn't Krista?"

"Shush, Tyler." She swats the side of his head and looks up at me. "He's asleep." Then she looks at me for another second and reads the calamity behind my eyes.

"I'll go wake him."

Jake's mom and brother have disappeared somewhere else in the house by the time Jake walks out, his hair mussed and his eyes bleary. He wears only a pair of boxers.

"What's up?" he asks in a drowsy voice. "Everything okay?"

"Can I talk to you?" My voice is still tiny and he strains to hear me.

"Sure." He looks around. "Let's go out back."

He leads me out the backdoor to the side of a swimming pool and pulls me down on its deck next to him. His feet dangle in the water. He puts an arm around me and draws me close.

"What's up?" he asks again.

"When I first got my learner's permit, I wanted to drive everywhere. Everywhere. My mom and dad always let me and it was a big deal in the family, really. At least it was to me. It made me feel grown up and important."

Jake looks at me with eyes that say *go on*. He nods.

"I always wanted to fill up the gas tank too. That was part of it. Stupid really, but every time the tank got down to even three-quarters full I'd pull into a gas station and make everyone wait while I filled it up. Then Lucy wanted to do it. She was too young to drive, and I guess that was her way of being part of the exciting event—my transition to adulthood. She wanted to experience that feeling too. And all that she could do was fill up the gas tank."

"Your sister . . . Lucy."

"But I was too jealous of the whole stupid thing. I wanted it to be about me, not her. And I got mad and told my mom I was the one who was driving, and I was the one who should pump the gas. It's so idiotic I can't even believe that I said it. So that day . . . that day . . . I was doing something after school and my mom and Lucy were driving somewhere and they stopped to buy gas. I know they didn't need it because I just filled the tank the day before. But Mom was probably trying to let Lucy have a turn, and since I wasn't there they stopped at the gas station so Lucy could pump the gas."

Jake knows what's coming next. He leans over and puts his other arm around me and holds me tight. I bury my head into his bare chest and the numbness is gone. I start to cry, but not sobbing—just crying like a springtime rain feels before the summer comes.

"If they hadn't been standing in that spot on that day, they'd still be alive. And all because I was so selfish I couldn't let my little sister pump the stupid gas into the stupid car."

Jake lets me cry and doesn't say anything. He just holds me. After a few minutes, he speaks.

"Hey, that's how it is with brothers and sisters. We act like idiots and learn to get along. It's how we figure stuff out. It's how we grow up."

"I know you're right, but . . ."

"I pushed my brother down the stairs once, fighting over a matchbox car. He broke his collarbone."

"You didn't kill him."

"And you didn't kill Lucy either."

WHEN I LEAVE Jake's house, he has only a few hours to sleep before boarding the bus to his football camp.

"It's okay," he says. "I can sleep on the bus just as well as I can sleep in my bed." I don't really believe him but I love him for saying it.

We didn't really talk much. His mother came out after a while to say good night and ask if there was anything we needed. I saw the way she looked at Jake . . . the same way Mom used to look at me when she could sense something was wrong but also knew that sometimes it was better to just stay in the background. It broke my heart to see that look . . . I so miss being the object of it. But it reassures me somehow that life goes on. And love goes on. I have to believe that it does.

Omar and I were loud enough to wake Rachel who sleeps with her window open. I know this because my father called me on my cell phone right after she ran to our house in her bare feet, ringing the doorbell over and over until she finally roused him from his sleep. He wanted to come get me, but I wasn't ready to leave Jake who I knew wouldn't talk if I didn't want to talk. Who wouldn't ask questions that I wasn't ready to answer. I just needed to be with Jake right then.

While I try explaining this to my father, I hear Grandpa in the background.

"Leave the girl," he says. "She will be fine. She will be back." And my father must believe him . . . and I believe him too.

When I get home, my father's bedroom light is on. I know he wants to see me, but I think he probably feels he should wait for me to come to him. Kind of like the way Jake's mom and my mom sometimes stayed in the background, right where we knew they'd be if we ever needed them. And I do need my dad . . . badly. He's been there with me all along, but I never realized it until tonight.

Instead of going to his room though, I walk down the hall. There, right across from the guest bedroom is the door that always stays closed. I open it and walk into the room where I feel Lucy's presence all around me.

The doll that Emma found is propped up on the pillow of Lucy's bed right where I left it. It stares straight ahead with its wide-eyed look of wonder, its loose auburn braid looking just like hers. Mom had been so surprised to come across this doll that day in the store—it so much resembled her younger daughter. And then, because I know that Lucy was a generous soul who shared everything with everybody, I pick up the doll that she had named Sarah. Lucy would want Emma to play with this doll. I know she would. It was only me who had to come around to accepting that fact. I shut off the lights and quietly close the door behind me as I leave her room.

Epilogue

My father and I finally came to our agreement—it only took us two years. I agreed to counseling if he would come with me, one last time, to the house at 758. And so, one morning we did just that. This time it was planned. We called ahead.

For people who like a happily ever after story, I wish I could say that we all felt happy and hugged and made up on that day but it didn't happen like that. We sat in the same room with nothing but silence between us. But when it was over we felt bound together, and in a strange way, we each had an interest in the happiness of the others.

As for the future, I'm pretty sure I can speak for the others when I say that, after that day, we were all more thankful for our greatest gift—the time we have remaining on earth.

Jake got back last week and Lyla gets home tomorrow. I've started seeing Dr. Bronstein again and it's difficult at times, but I know it's helpful. Summer already feels like it's winding down, but I'm excited at the thought of going back to school and watching my first football game from the stands. Jake's been teaching me the rules of the game.

I've started writing again and thinking seriously about college. Everything seems . . . at least possible. And, oh yeah, I've moved back into my bedroom although I keep my tent up on the roof for my private getaway. Once the rains start, it will have to come down.

Shortly after getting back from Disneyland, Marie moved out of the house. She got her own place and now shares custody of Chad and Emma with her ex-husband. Dad and Marie still see each other and I think they still love each other, but they both decided they rushed into something without thinking about the consequences to their kids. That's what Dad told me. Exactly that.

TONIGHT, I'M JUST enjoying an owl's eye view on this warm, cloudless night. I'll miss sitting up here once the weather turns cold, but Grandpa is coming to visit us for Thanksgiving, so I'm happy about that.

The day before he left we were sitting in the living room while he flipped through the pages of our coffee table book about the greatest works of art. He paused at the page on the Venus de Milo which is permanently displayed at the Louvre Museum in Paris. Carved out of marble before the birth of Christ, the statue depicts Aphrodite, the goddess of love and beauty.

"Look at this, Krista." My grandpa held up the glossy photo of the statue. "If someone will see this and notice only that the arms are broken, they would miss something beautiful and rare."

I looked at the picture, as if for the first time, even though I had seen it many times before—the wavy hair pulled back to expose a serene face of perfectly proportioned features; the careless slouch of a body, both feminine and powerful; the exquisite folds of fabric that could be silk instead of stone. But that day, for the first time, it was the imperfection of her missing arms that made this statue so compelling to me.

"May I see your list please?" He closed the book and set it down on the round, glass coffee table.

"I don't have a list anymore, Grandpa. Now that you're leaving."

He fumbled through his pockets and pulled out what looked like an old receipt written in Spanish. In another pocket, he found a pen. He wrote something on the receipt and then handed it to me.

"What's this?"

Scrawled across the top he had written:

See the Venus de Milo in Paris.

"It's my gift to you," he said. "The beginning of a new list. Now *you* must finish it yourself."

The chorus of crickets chirps in a steady, rhythmic beat. The celestial bodies above me sparkle and pulse. Once, a young Gyuri guided himself to happiness and safety using the position of these stars. Once, a young girl who was called Kicsi by the father who adored her, dreamed dreams under these stars. Once, two young sisters sneaked up to the roof of their garage and imagined each star to be a falling star that would make all their wishes come true.

. . . a million kisses . . . and a million more . . .

Acknowledgements

My deepest gratitude to Amberjack Publishing for believing in me and this story. Dayna Anderson, Kayla Church, Jenny Miller, and Cami Wasden—a dream team if there ever was one.

About the Author

Kathryn Berla is the author of YA romances, *12 Hours in Paradise* and *Dream Me*. *The House at 758* is an English translation of *La Casa 758*, which was originally published by Penguin Random House, Spain.

Kathryn graduated from the University of California Berkeley with a degree in English, but she takes the most pride in having studied creative writing under Walter van Tilburg Clark at the University of Nevada.

Kathryn lives with her husband in the beautiful San Francisco Bay Area, which she would never leave because she can't think of another place with as much to offer, including the proximity of her entire family.